WELCOME
TO ANOTHER

CRYSTAL LAKE PUBLISHING
CREATION

Join today at www.crystallakepub.com & www.patreon.com/CLP

Subscribe to Crystal Lake Publishing's
Dark Tide series for updates, specials,
behind-the-scenes content, and a
special selection of bonus stories
- http://eepurl.com/hKVGkr

Our Dark Tide series of novella anthologies

DARK TIDE

THE DEATHPLACE SET

KAARON WARREN

ITS A COMPLICATED STORY, but bear with me.

My dad was once a charming man. There wasn't a soul who didn't love him. He was the one who went into school if any of us got into trouble, especially if it was a female teacher. We moved around a lot. Lots of schools, lots of teachers. He had this way of leaning forward and of disagreeing in such an agreeable way they thought he was agreeing. He was a chameleon, changing to match anyone around him. That all gives a tone to this I hadn't intended. A flippancy and a cleverness with words, when all I want to do is write the history of the cigarette cards and how they killed all of us.

Sorry. Flippant again.

We've still got Mum and I'm not, in fact, dead, and neither is Joy, although she has a clear, self-medicated death wish nobody can ease her from. She's having a good time and no one can stop her from enjoying oblivion. And of course without those cigarette cards, Mum and Dad would never have met (it was *impossible* they would have met) and we wouldn't have been here in the first place.

CARD 2/24
THE BEAR'S HEAD, CANBERRA

Built in 1872, it was licensed soon after as an inn, providing a stop between two trading posts until 1888, when a brawl broke out in the beer garden. While this was not uncommon at the time, with tired men drinking too much strong liquor, this incident resulted in the deaths of eight, including two women and a child of five. It began, they say, when a game of billiards got out of hand, and one man thought he would make his point with his cue across the face of the serving girl. The worst of it, people said for years later, is that the victims were left to bleed to death, every man leaving at a run. The inn closed down for fifty years, by which time the deaths were long forgotten and the blood long since faded.

A hundred years later, the beer garden was different but the same. The stones were more worn and had been re-grouted. The shed had been turned into the pool room, and people could stand outside and look in. It was a crappy old table, destined for the rubbish, so no one minded it sitting out here in the converted shed.

━╱╿╲━

Jarrold was a skinny thing the day Gloria met him. The night. The morning? It was past midnight, for sure, and the din of the pub had mutated into a kind of buzz. He was in the pool room, knocking the wrong balls into the wrong holes on purpose, to make people laugh, because he was too small to defend himself in a fight and people didn't pick one if you made people laugh.

Later, much later, decades later, he was bigger in every way. Taller, wider, heavier. Fights? Defending himself? He loved a fight; he used to be a loser, later he could win if he picked the right opponent. The ones with no imagination were harder to beat because they didn't see the weirdness of shifting surfaces, or the ghosts themselves.

Gloria didn't notice him at first. She stood by herself in the beer garden, in the back corner where the bodies had been piled a hundred years earlier. No one remembered now. Almost no one.

"They say if you're here when the place is empty, you can hear the last breaths of the dying. All of them together, like . . . " Jarrold took a deep breath and let it *whoosh* out. He had his arms full of dirty glasses. Break was over. He had work to do behind the bar.

She watched him walk away, then flicked through the small pack of cards she held.

"Buy you a drink?" This man was far handsomer, but his face was bland and she knew for sure he'd never mimic the dying breath of ghosts.

"I'll get my own," she said, and she walked to the bar, hearing the inevitable *'Bitch'* behind her. Jarrold gave her a particularly full glass of wine but didn't wink at her, which she appreciated.

Back in the beer garden, she sat with her wine and her cards.

"Porno?" Jarrold asked her, smiling as he cleared tables.

"No! And not tarot either." She showed him Card 2—this pub— and, once he'd finished work, she told him the story of the cards and how, while there were 24 of them, she had never managed to list them because they seemed to change each time she tried.

3

He took the cards from her and felt a wave of nausea. He told her later that was the moment he fell in love, that he felt ill with love almost at first sight. She waited until his shift was over and they sat in the dark together, listening to each other breathe, both certain they could hear that ghostly breathing as well.

Every relationship, be it friendship or romance, starts because of a wild number of coincidences.

CARD 3/24
DRYDEN RAILWAY STATION, NSW

Every day thousands (millions) of people travel through railways stations, each of them carrying their own story. Sometimes those stories end at the station; deliberately or not falling in front of a train: heart attack, violent attack, robbery—random or otherwise.

This card depicts a badly vandalized station, long since closed down. The death depicted here (of one of the local unfortunates who stumbled onto the tracks) occurred in 1890, and brought new regulations to railway platforms across Australia.

Gloria showed Jarrold Card 3 as they stood by his car, which had one wheel almost mired in a deep pothole. He held her hand as they stepped up onto a platform covered with graffiti and pickaxe holes, as if someone had been looking for treasure, or for a body. He was sweating slightly, and he thought it was a bit chemical, perhaps from the super-strong deodorant he'd used.

"I think Dad would have chucked himself in front of a train here if they were running. Just for the irony or whatever of it. He did it in Yass, though. Near home."

She gave him a quick look at Card 15, 'Home on the Back Streets of a Country Town'.

"Can you feel it? A tear in the place? Damage done," Gloria said.

They held hands, quiet, and listened for it. A rustling sound, or a shuffling, as if someone very tired walked barefoot just out of sight.

Some families are evil. Some have evil thrust upon them.

CARD 15/24
HOME ON THE BACKSTREETS OF A COUNTRY TOWN

From the outside, this house appears ordinary. Certainly it would not cause a passer-by to stop and comment. Inside, though, all the walls are stripped of plaster, and the cross-beamed planks once held a variety of trinkets. These have not been changed since 1960, when an apparent witch lived here, attaching great importance to each item in the walls. The woman (described as 'old' in the press but who in fact was only 35) was attacked by locals when one of their children went missing. Her hands were removed and her throat cut, and she was left to die on the floor of this house. The child was found soon after, playing with the doll she had stolen, and this house has passed from hand to hand since.

"My father moved here once Mum divorced him," Gloria said. "None of us had any idea why this place until I got hold of the cards." She looked at Card 15 again and handed it to Jarrold when he reached for it. "He was never the same after my uncle Rufus died, and he was a bastard before that, anyway. But after Uncle Rufus died, and Dad got left nothing at all, he turned on my mother as if she was ruining his life. Good on her for dumping him. He basically spent the rest of his life travelling the country, with this place left empty most of the time."

"Was Rufus the good brother?" Jarrold asked, partly joking.

"No! He was awful. He used to pinch us. If he picked you up, you'd be covered in bruises. Everyone loved him though. He was good on the banjo." She strummed an imaginary one.

Jarrold half rose out of his seat as if he could protect her from this, way in the past.

"After Dad's funeral, I had to come here and get it all sorted. He had friends, neighbors, three daughters, a son, and a sister-in-law who'd always fancied him. But I'm the one who did it."

The house was neat, clean and organized, with no expired food in the cupboard or fridge, no unwashed plates, no old scraps under the couch or the bed. This was a meticulous man, terminally ill or not. His liver cancer was only discovered after his death, making it clear how deliberate the fall in front of the train was.

He was not the type to have his body left unfound, but the house stank as if his corpse had sat there for weeks. He loved to be loved; the pain he inflicted was on strangers, so he never had to suffer the consequences.

"He didn't inflict pain on any of us. He didn't like consequences, something he'd learned at a young age, walking home from school with a younger, extremely annoying neighbor. He told us this story over and over. He had taken the opportunity to send that boy into a front yard which, he knew, was guarded by unrestrained dogs.

"'They always leave beer for the postman,' my dad said. 'On the front step. Go and get it and we'll drink it together.'

"'I'm not the postman,' the stupid boy said.

"So my dad thrust a sheet of notepaper into his hand. 'It's a love letter,' he told him. 'Go on. Deliver it.'

"Of course it was just a sheet of notepaper, and there was no beer, and the boy's injuries after being attacked by the dog had him out of school for weeks. My dad wasn't punished because nothing could be proven or even spoken about, but for a while people looked at him differently, warily, until they eventually forgot."

After that Gloria's father took his pleasures further afield. His death was testimony to that, afflicting trauma on the train driver and the observers—particularly the young woman who saw him too close to the edge but did not want to go near him, let alone touch him.

That smell.

"I was the one sent in to sort his house out. Youngest daughter, no family of my own, job not career, nothing better to do. 'You're not as sensitive,' our aunt said—something they all believed, because in contrast to my weepy, mother-of-five, loyal sister, I was the cold one. The police had tried to find the source of the smell. To me it was vaguely familiar, perhaps something from childhood, perhaps (and this thought would have made my sister scream) it was the smell of our grandmother dying."

She remembered the stink of it rising, now that his smell (of soap, of Old Spice, of onions frying) was fading. Insensitive or not, she'd followed her nose to his study. Dark, small, cramped. Not musty, though. Ventilation was always good in that house. The floor was concrete so there was nothing caught under the floorboards to make that smell. There was only a desk, a filing cabinet and a small cupboard that sat in the room, all surfaces clear but dusty now. No rodent pawprints to show her there might be dead mice in the walls. Following her nose, she opened the small cupboard. The local police had been through the house looking for a suicide note to confirm their assessment and yes, he'd left one here, taped to his filing cabinet, saying that he didn't want to be a burden and also that the ghosts were too loud now. Thinking of those words had made her ears hum and buzz, as if a dozen voices chattered in the lounge room; a friendly party she wasn't invited to. But of course no one was there. Her nostrils flared. The smell was definitely worse here. When she opened the cupboard door it hit her in a waft. She covered her mouth and nose with her shirt and peered in.

There were a series of black briefcases, a dozen or more, stacked on top of one another. Labelled *Property of Duncan Airlie*. And *1880, 1890, 1891*—and more.

On top was an exercise book with her father's vividly recognizable handwriting. *'Cigarette Cards Issues 1880-1940'* and *'This is true of all collecting. It extinguishes the moral instinct. The object finally possesses the possessor.'* ~ *John Fowles*

Inside the cases were hundreds and hundreds of cigarette cards. There was dried lavender in each case, to keep the earwigs and mold away. The last suitcase contained a small box and, opening it, she understood this was where the smell came from.

"But there was nothing inside but these cards," she told Jarrod now, "and a note that said *Found in the arms of a long-dead woman*." She shuddered. "He always did love a good creepy story, my dad. God knows where he really did get them. I hate to think."

Jarrold sniffed them and recoiled.

The cards were old, and she'd thought she might get some money for them so, smell notwithstanding, she piled them into her car. There was little else of value in the place, not even photographs or any of their mother's jewelry. There were no souvenirs of his travels; no knickknacks, no t-shirts, no snow globes. He used to send them postcards, although they noticed over time that the pictures rarely matched the stamps or the post office markings, as if he was racing to get ahead of himself. She did take all of his books, including his remarkable true crime collection.

It was a five-hour drive back home. The smell was fainter, but the buzzing in her ears was stronger (this must have been tiredness) and she kept glimpsing shadows in the seat next to her, as well as in the rearview mirror. Her backseat was filled with the briefcases, the books in the boot. With every movement she imagined spiders crawling out of the briefcases. She'd only quickly checked them all; a nest could easily be hiding.

Chiding herself, she drove home.

Gloria always told her stories like this.

"I didn't unpack the car when I arrived past midnight. I'd eaten hamburgers on the way so I wasn't hungry, just very thirsty. I parked outside under a streetlight (a precaution Dad had always insisted on) and headed up to my apartment. There were only six in my block. All of them were silent in the dark night, although I could hear the faint thump of a sleep breathing machine thingy from number two. On very still nights I could see and hear this thump from my place, but it didn't disturb me. Rather, I found it comforting. I didn't like it when it stopped. I slept in the next day. It was overcast and misty; when I glanced out at my car it seemed shrouded, although the mist had dispersed by the time I headed downstairs. Some of it was trapped in the car, I thought, because inside it swirled and blurred. I felt a vacuum suck of air as I opened the back door.

"My sister Dannie stood waiting. She didn't like the hard work but was there for the spoils. I said, *Give me a hand to get Dad's things upstairs.* She swung two bottles of prosecco and said, *Hand full!* So typical of her. I called her a lazy boozy cow and she actually helped.".

In the end it took the two of them to heft the five suitcases, the four shopping bags of books, the cardboard box of top-shelf alcohol and the small box of Waterford Crystal, a wedding present their parents had never used.

Dannie wrinkled her nose and poked out her tongue. 'Bit stinky,' she said. 'You might want to air these on your balcony before you take them inside.'

It was a good idea. The mist was gone and the sun was out, so they wouldn't get damp out there. They stacked them and poured bubbles into the fancy wine glasses.

'So what's in the cases?' Danni asked.

'Believe it or not, cigarette cards.'

They opened one case. Inside each set (Film Stars and Their Pets; Beauty Spots of Britain; Railway Engines; so many more) was secured with a piece of ribbon, and a small paper note listing the missing cards.

Dannie picked up a card and sniffed it, then recoiled. 'That's your stink.'

━╱┃╲━

Dannie and her family moved overseas soon after this. Gloria missed them.

━╱┃╲━

"The set was called The Deathplace Set," Gloria told Jarrold. "These cards were produced later than the rest. A special set. I'm not sure how many places my dad tracked down, but the pub was my third, after here and the railway station."

Jarrold picked up the set. They were clammy. Stained in some places. He could feel the blood rushing through his veins, could hear it, and he felt more alive than he ever had.

"So wait, you still own this house? It's yours?"

She nodded.

"We need to do this thing up and sell the crap out of it," he said.

Over the next few months, they tore up the rotting floorboards and laid down a new one. They crawled on their hands and knees, looking for some sign, some memory of the witchy woman who'd died there. When Jarrold felt a splinter thrust into the meat of his thumb, he thought this was perhaps a message, that this flooring needed to be destroyed to remove all trace of the death. The splinter proved hard to remove, until it turned septic and pus pushed it out.

They replastered the walls, which minimized but never removed altogether the sound of wind whistling through the house. They left the myriad of items in the walls, superstitious enough to feel anxious about removing them.

━╱┃╲━

This was the first of the death houses they flipped.

Sometimes vandalism is in the details.

CARD 16/24
SELF-SUFFICIENT HOLIDAY HOME, BYRON BAY

This self-sufficient holiday home uses no new materials. Every element is repurposed, from the reclaimed wood for the floorboards to the rescued glass for the windows. It's an open-plan house, lots of ways for the breeze to flow through, fresh off the ocean. There is no sign of the hushed-up bloody mayhem that took place here in 1961. A local leader of the community invited a houseful of guests, and in a psychotic episode killed them all after taking some bad drugs. One body was found in the compost. It isn't there now, of course. But there are stories of the fingerbones sticking out like pale fungi. The killer died by his own hand, leaving behind a note explaining that his victims were all evil spirits, possessed, or witches.

Gloria had thought she'd never marry. Never fall in love. It was the obsession; the cigarette cards and what they meant to her—this set in particular, innocuous looking, but the descriptions on the back . . . and yet Jarrold became as obsessed as she was. When they discovered the Byron Bay house still stood, he said, "We should go there for our honeymoon," and that was how he proposed.

It was a small wedding. They drove straight from the registry office to Byron Bay, an eight-hour journey. They took turns driving and being passenger, and both tried to keep the conversation going but it was a test of the fact that they barely knew each other, and that what they had in common were those cards.

The house itself was lovely. It was meant to be self-sufficient, but of course the solar panels were malfunctioning, the water tank almost empty and brackish, and the garden and compost were overrun with weeds and rats.

They lay in bed that first night (and yes, that was the night their oldest child was conceived) with the windows open, an ocean breeze dancing over them and the sound of the waves gentle and calming. Still, they knew what had happened here. They couldn't see it, but they knew it. If there were ghosts, those ghosts were quiet, and if there was a curse it settled on them as gently as that breeze.

Is this where it really started? This honeymoon in Byron Bay, poisoned by the old wood, haunted and then enriched by the ghosts?

CARD 9/24
OLD CORNER SHOP, OUTER SUBURBS

Once a busy and profitable shop, it fell into disrepair in the 1930s. Patrons believed the owner to be a man of two faces, and they never knew which one they would get: charming or irritable. It was only years later they realized there were in fact two men, brothers, and that one had murdered the other in a fit of rage and greed. Stripping the place clean, he left his brother lying in the backroom where a squatter, desperate for a place to sleep, eventually broke in and discovered it. By this stage the body was dried up and barely noticeable, and so the shop became a haunt for drifters for many years, and the body was left as part of the furniture.

Jarrold found this place, Card 9 (A Grand Opportunity for Improvement), and went to see it, leaving the heavily pregnant Gloria at home. It was time to sell up and move on, and this place was perfect. Falling apart, apparently haunted, it had been on the market for years, dropping in value day by day. It was going *"cheap-cheap-cheap"*. It had potential, though.

"Bloody vandals," the real estate guy said. He lived at the local pub, and was round, red and sweaty. "Look, I'll be honest with ya," (but he wasn't; he said nothing about the murder), "it's had a rough couple of years. The drinkers'll head up here when the pub shuts, carry on for a bit. At least they're out of harm's way but I'm not saying they don't leave a mark."

At least they didn't shit inside; someone had dug a hole in the backyard and that's where they went. It was badly vandalized, with obscenities scrawled throughout, unwanted items left in cupboards and corners, dirty clothing everywhere (including an inordinate amount of women's underwear).

"Cheap-cheap-cheap, Mr Carstairs!" the real estate guy said, not really expecting to make the sale, but he did.

Gloria, Jarrold and the baby (Joy, the first of five) moved in two months later. The place was a disaster but they got to work straight away, converting the downstairs to a kitchen, lounge and play area, the top floor to bedrooms and a bathroom. Work went smoothly, only interrupted by locals at times. They'd used it as a party house for years because it had been vacant for so long, and it was hard for them to get used to it being occupied. They'd kick the door in if he locked it, but Jarrold was already stronger, already bigger with whatever it was that built him up, and a few solid beatings kept them away in the future. He was wiry still, wearing big boots, shorts, paint everywhere, a neat haircut. Gloria was tired with the baby but exhilarated to be living in this place.

They had a lot of sex in that house.

Martin was born, then Maurice soon after, born close together, names foolishly similar. No one could ever tell them apart.

━╱╿╲━

They were having sex downstairs to avoid the children when Gloria noticed a Peeping Tom in the window. Jarrold chased after with nothing but a pillow covering him, and the man disappeared up the backyard. Gloria and Jarrold laughed so hard they woke the children. It was a light moment, but it helped them realize it was time to move, to finish the renovations and sell for profit. The corner shop was on a main road, far too dangerous with young children—and besides, it was renovated and beautiful and worth three times what they'd bought it for.

They put up a joke sign saying *'No ghosts here'*, and that got the punters in. In truth, they sometimes smelled a cheap aftershave no longer sold, and sometimes heard mumbling that didn't come from any of their frequent pub visitors.

What gain was there in tracking all the deathplaces down? Morbid curiosity? I think motivation changed as time went by. Early on, it was for the money. Buying places with a bad reputation and selling them at a great profit. Dad was in it for the big bucks, the easy money. They weren't the first to own the cards, or to want to visit every deathplace, but they were the first to monetize it. Then we came and left and vanished, and perhaps he was trying to track us down by tracking down ghosts?

He believed that by his very presence at each deathplace he could complete a circle. He was not a religious man (although dragged us to church week after week until one by one we rebelled), and yet he always had a prayer of comfort to offer. And he always left something behind. It was rarely anything of his, let's be clear. More like a bracelet belonging to one of the children. On two occasions, children themselves.

And he swore there was always a sign of some kind, a scratch or a mark, an indication only he could sometimes see.

CARD 7/24
WEATHERBOARD HOUSE, WERRIBEE, MELBOURNE

'Glorious exterior at a bargain price.'

Such a pretty house on the outside! But so dark inside, with the built-in, covered verandah, tiled front and back, many of those tiles cracked and broken, every crack telling a story of heavy footfall or dropped items. The only known deaths occurred during the construction, when a wall collapsed and three men died, with four more severely injured. Interestingly, all of them were newly married, none of them fathers, and so it could be said that this house meant the end of the line for them.

The deaths were so long ago there was not even a hint of them, and yet nightly Jarrold would go into the basement and lie on the dirt there, until Gloria insisted he lay down an old carpet and she joined him, and they listened for the sound of scratching, the soft sigh of tired men seeking release.

—✦—

She had Leeanne here, which delighted Joy. A sister at last, after two smelly little brothers. Gloria said enough, four is enough. In the basement, the sighing rose. Gloria ventured down there, Leeanne in her arms, Martin (or was it Maurice?) holding on to her pants leg, because it sounded as if a dying animal was trapped and she would release it.

Leeanne was a quiet baby, luckily, because Maurice was sickly and needy.

"Mum," the boy said, pointing. "Who's that?"

She saw nothing more than a shimmering, perhaps a shine on the ground, but that was enough to terrify her and in an awful instinct, she held the baby in front of her face as she and the boy backed up the stairs to get away. They subsided, sank back.

Jarrold stretched out supine on the slate tiles in the basement, fingers and toes pointing to the four corners. He came back glowing, as if he had absorbed a sense of power. He had the sort of glow that led to baby making, and sure enough, Gloria fell pregnant.

These stories are all we heard.

Our lives were built around these places.

CARD 20/24
A HOUSE WITH FIVE VERY SMALL BEDROOMS, ON THE EDGE OF A FOREST

Structurally unsound, this house was once a solid three-bedroom home with a small living area. It was converted by the cult that took it over; five small bedrooms, a large gathering area, bathroom space converted to look like a public toilet, with stainless steel and white tiles. They slept three or four to a room and used the big communal areas for praying and sharing blessed food.

A 'midden' stood on the edge of the forest, where they buried all the food scraps, tins, and wrappings, as if scared someone might use them for witchcraft purposes. Hair and clothing were buried there too.

They hated witches and believed the only escape was heaven, where witches didn't go.

They'd gather herbs and mushrooms they found at the base of trees. They believed their god would look after them.

They made an enormous pot of mushroom and tarragon soup one day. Some died in the shared area, some in the bedrooms. The one who died out in the forest wasn't found for a few weeks. The corpse was picked clean by then, only bones left. The weird thing was, the bones were all lined up like a small white picket fence.

Rhiannon was the only one of them considered a mistake and they never let her forget it, in that way that families have of showing love.

They couldn't fit beds into the bedrooms, just single mattresses. There was no room for wardrobes. All their stuff had to be out in the massive common areas, the 'unique living areas for families who like to spend time together'.

"This is a ridiculous house," Joy said, and that became the name of the house: *Chateau Ridiculous.*

"You wait and see how much money we make," Jarrold said. He was still ordinary sized back then, although starting to stretch out of his clothes.

The carpet was bad. Sticky, clumpy, stained. That was the first thing to go. Underneath, the floorboards were disappointing. Not hardwood, and stained with some kind of liquid. The children took to camping out in the forest a lot, to escape the stuffiness inside. Mushrooms still grew; they were warned not to touch them, let alone eat them.

The Carstairs children loved this forest, as did all their friends, and they'd invite a dozen people over to play war games and pretend to be lost.

We moved around a lot when I was a kid. We'd leave a place quickly. I always forgot something, leaving behind a trail of teddy bears, books, cardigans, shoes, and once, a dental retainer.

We never went back.

CARD 19/24
CUBBY HOUSE/PLAY HOUSE AT
PRESCHOOL/KINDERGARTEN

Built at the same time as the preschool was built, using the leftover materials, the cubby house is a masterful example of small architecture. It mirrors the larger building precisely, provides shelter from the sun, and has enough windows that no child need fear the dark.

It was a temptation, though for teenagers with beer and for vandals who loved wrecking play equipment. Who knew why? And, on one occasion, for a man so drunk he thought this was a good hiding place for the body of the wife he'd just beaten within an inch of her life. Here, in this small space, she gave up.

They'd caught the killer red-handed, thanks to a neighbor who always kept an eye on the school.

Rhiannon was ready to go to preschool, although her siblings all tried to terrify her about it. They told her people would make fun of her and that she would starve because they would steal her lunch.

Gloria said, "Stop it."

Jarrold was filling out papers. He wanted her to go to a different school; he wanted access to that cubby house. He didn't care that they were out of the area; he had bought a tiny one-bedroom apartment so he had something to put on the forms.

"Just let her go to the same school as the others," Gloria said. He seemed larger; she felt weaker.

"I've heard a good thing about this preschool," he said. He waved something at her.

"The local is perfectly fine," she said, although none of their kids had gone there.

"Who says?" He didn't pause to hear her answer. "Look, we've got a bright one here."

Rhiannon made herself as small as possible, hoping they'd forget she was there and say nice things about her.

Maurice came barreling in, knocking over a vase and spilling slightly stagnant water all over the table. The smell made Gloria feel sick.

"We can walk to the local in minutes. This one is a thirty-minute drive away. It makes no sense, Jarrold."

"I'll take her," he said.

And he did, each school day. He volunteered to help in the mornings, and when they all trusted him, he told them stories in the cubby house. It became a favorite part of the day. He squatted and waddled through the doorway like a duck, even then having to tilt his head so he didn't bang it. The children followed suit, quacking, flapping, laughing, falling over. His own daughter quacked front and center, and in that moment he loved his proud, rowdy girl even more.

They were all so chattery, fidgety, and noisy, he could get no sense of anything in the cubby house. But he knew that, beneath the linoleum, nailed down, there was a bloodstain the size of a child.

He told a story to the children, full of wild movements that made them flinch and laugh. He closed his eyes, trying to hear below all that, to the terrible thing that must have happened here.

I remember that cubby house very clearly.

CARD 5/24
LARGE, OLD, RED SUBURBAN HOUSE, COBURG, MELBOURNE

Set in the center of two ordinary blocks, this two-story home of red brick was built in 1902 and has been renovated many times since. The layers of wallpaper lay testament to this. There is a huge garden all around. Roses, geraniums, herbs, leeks, pomegranate, succulents.

The man died at the front door in 1922, scrabbling for keys, the alarm for jail break pealing, him panicking, just keeled over. If it had happened ten minutes later he would have been inside and perhaps joined the ranks of the long-dead unfound. Haunted, they say. Lots of people have rented this place for short periods only. He rattles the keys. You can hear it at night.

The joy of moving in to this place! This 'unprecedented in size and history' house!

Joy took the best bedroom, no arguments, with everyone else falling into place after her. Most of the garden was dying, so the family put all the plants in pots on the front curb for people to take for free. They all took great pleasure in stripping back the wallpaper, year after year after year revealed. If they were hoping for a message, they didn't get one. It felt like vandalism to tear off the paper this way, but the walls underneath would look good painted a rose pink to match the bricks outside; Jarrold was sure they'd add fifty thousand at least with this simple improvement.

—⁄|\—

This house, with its rumor of haunting, and living in the shadow of the enormous greystone jail, would not increase in value without intervention. But it was a bargain-basement price and "had good bones". If they had to live with sirens and alarms and, on a still day, the shouts of the imprisoned men, that was fine. There was a small backyard, big enough for a blowup swimming pool, and the family was happy here for a while.

Jarrold liked to sit on the front step where the man had died. It was not his imagination that he took strength from this place; he really did.

There were dozens of deaths in the prison itself, from the official to the riotous, the *blessed relief* to the *taken too soon*. Gloria signed up as an official visitor to have the excuse to get behind those walls and suck up the atmosphere. She was tired from the children and the moves and all of it; as Jarrold gained strength, she seemed to lose hers.

Gloria came back from the jail flushed with good works. Her visits ended when there was an outbreak of virulent flu and she couldn't afford to get sick; neither did she want the children to fall ill.

—⁄|\—

The prison shadow over them wasn't a bother at all, and they grew used to the bells, timing their own lives around them. Joy developed romantic ideas about the men inside, as if they would break out and rescue her from her family, and she would sit in the backyard sunbathing in the hope she would be seen, safe in the knowledge she wouldn't be.

Jarrold got the children to help smash the tiles on the front verandah and they did it with squealing delight.

—⁄|\—

They stayed here for the longest time so far. They loved that big old house. Plenty of room for all and a big backyard so they could have a dog like ordinary people.

I never quite understood why we did it, at least not until the cards were mine. Some people cut themselves to let the sorrow out, others destroy things. Slash tires, scrawl graffiti, smash windows. We did those things to let the ghosts out.

CARD 11/24
THE ZOO

Built in 1912, this zoo has undergone changes over the years. First established as a place for wild animals, it now houses tamer breeds after a number of unfortunate incidents, all noted in the illustration. The lion's den, 1949, almost caused the zoo to be closed as a young girl somehow climbed into the enclosure and was devoured before her parents even noticed. There is no record of what happened to the lions on this occasion.

The children understood about the cards by now and had decided they needed to be photographed, holding the card, in front of the lion's den—which was now a penguin enclosure.

When asked where her father got the cards, Gloria claimed not to know, but from the smell of the cards and the way she changed the subject, everyone knew she had more information than she was providing.

"Have you found the mark?" she asked Jarrold, who was peering in through the rungs.

"I can't see one." He liked to find a literal mark, something he could collect and control. He reached through into the enclosure for a flat grey rock, streaked with a shiny red. "This, perhaps," he said.

All families think they are ordinary until they realize they aren't.

CARD 4/24
WOODEN BRIDGE, REINFORCED

Built in 1888 as part of the Melbourne Expo celebrations, the bridge serviced foot traffic as well as carriages for many years. It now stands as an occasional roadway, and while it has the appearance of age, it has been shored up underneath to the extent that 'you could drive a ten-ton truck over it'. Surprisingly, it has been the scene of few suicides or accidents, given the enticing rush of the river below. It is known, though, that a father threw his five-year-old daughter over in 1890, and this act has been copied periodically ever since.

On the way home to their beloved red house, Jarrold took the long way, over Valencia Bridge, even though the children were tired. Joy was well over family time and wanted to get home to talk to her boyfriend in private. This was one of Jarrold's favorite bridges; here a man had thrown his daughter over, but not himself, and Jarrold was sure that the minute that man died, his ghost would be here trying to save his poor innocent child. Gloria stood high on a railing, stretching over further than she should. Below, the water crashed and splashed tiny water droplets on her cheeks. In that moment she was unutterably happy.

Jarrold lifted Rhiannon up, feeling her weight, feeling her hang on in absolute trust, and his throat constricted in a sob. There was no understanding it.

Jarrold put her down again and began his search. He was certain that every death left a literal mark behind, regardless of how death occurred. A symbol, or a divot in the road. An odd pile of rocks that wasn't there before. Markings on a wall. He leant over the bridge but the water was too deep; he'd have to get down there and dive to find the place the poor girl died. Most people would say there was no sign that the death occurred, that if you didn't know what happened there, you'd never guess. That you couldn't pinpoint the spot by looking.

Jarrold took photos but also ripped away all the bits he thought held the mark. He made the children help; tearing off strips of paint, removing a screw. They'd do this going forward, leaving their mark. They'd be called vandals by most, but is it vandalism if there is a point to it? If they left behind holes in walls and floors, and damaged furniture?

☛ ⟋ ⟍ ⟍

On the side of the bridge someone has painted 'RIP Precious Girl'. They piled into the car and headed home. Tired. They tracked the trip via landmarks that had become familiar. The tree struck by lightning and never removed. The billboard covered with badly painted penises. The house with a dozen old cars parked out the front. All of these led them home. Martin said, "They should do a card set of *Nearly-Home Landmarks*," and that was when their one and only family game was born: inventing other silly card sets. All the children loved looking through the cigarette cards, hundreds of them, and sorting and re-sorting.

☛ ⟋ ⟍ ⟍

The car shuddered as Jarrold pulled into their driveway. It was due to be replaced, but he had a great affection for this one. Cars like it were hard to find; mostly they ended up at the wreckers. This one had been driven into the water by a man who then abandoned his wife to die. Oddly enough, his father had committed suicide in the same car, and there were ridges of the father's blood still under the mats. Not now, of course. The river water washed them away.

Any number of bridges would do. In fact any bridge of a certain height is sure to carry a death of one kind or another.

CARD 23/24
CAFÉ, COOLANGATTA, QLD

Built in 1920 on the site where the old mail coaches used to stop between Sydney and Brisbane. At the time no expense was spared, and this is evident now; the fittings and the structure itself are as sound as a hundred years ago. With pink tiles covering the floor and a third of the walls, ornate and solid iron railings, metal and Formica tables and a long steel bench, this café remains a testament to style and taste.

The place was called The Coachhouse, for the old coach that sat at the back of the café. This was the last of the coaches that ran from Yuleba to St George, and sitting inside it you could still smell the man who last rode inside it. Any number of artists of varying degrees of talent have painted this very coach. One such painting hangs on the wall of the small outdoor toilet. In it, four horses draw the carriage. Two or three men sit on the platform; it is hard to tell. One is perhaps a ghost. It's an enclosed wagon, piled high on top with deliveries. Parcels and letters. Who is inside the carriage, or is it all parcels in there as well? A moving crime scene. An easy way to transport a murder victim. And the coach abandoned somewhere. Where are they all? The old Cobb and Co. coaches. Destroyed? Fallen apart? In someone's backyard or shed? Filled with hundreds of generations of mouse droppings and mice and other creatures.

The café sits on the main street of town. It has very pretty blue-painted balustrades and window frames. Lovely flowerboxes on the second floor. A beautifully wrought iron sign, still in perfect condition, says 'Welcome to the Coachhouse'.

The murder depicted on this card occurred in 1971 when the passions of the kitchen overtook two chefs. Her husband discovered them easily and, being a farmer, he had easy access to a gun. They say the resulting bloodbath took weeks to clean up, with the end result being the kitchen fully replaced. Since then the café has passed through many hands.

Jarrold sat with a newspaper in front of him. The house was empty, everybody out doing things that didn't involve him. He laid out the cards, shaking his head, placing them all next to each other in a grid.

He stared at them.

He piled all of them up except one. Card 23. Café. This he laid next to the newspaper, which showed a colorful, badly taken photograph of a café for sale.

This café. *'Thriving business with great potential for motivated owners.'*

━ノ۱➤━

When the family got home, he showed Gloria the card. "Do you remember this one?"

She shook her head. "Did you make it? You've done a good job."

"I didn't make it," he said.

He didn't care about the house they lived in as much as the others did. All along the idea had been to fix it up, sell it, move on. It was fixed; verandah modernized, garden perfect, walls and floors improved, cupboards updated. Roof replaced. The café carried a house with it, and a granny flat, and the café itself would be theirs. It wasn't something Gloria and Jarrold had considered before, but it was tempting. The children were getting older and they could work and help out, gaining experience and confidence. Gloria loved to cook; she could set up a small bakery and sell cakes. Jarrold liked to be amongst lively people, and he missed his days working in the pub.

In the end, they let the cards decide, as they had done for some years now. It was 'written in the cards' Jarrold said, a joke that was neither clever nor funny but perhaps inevitable.

─╱┃╲─

Gloria was ready. She liked the idea of a new deathplace, she liked the idea of having a café to create, and thought it would be good for the children to start jobs. They told Joy she could be the head waiter if she wanted, or she could learn how to cook; anything. That drew her in. Plus she was tired of life in the suburbs, and this café was close to the beach and just on the outskirts of the city. They bundled the kids into the van and took off, stopping along the way at motels (flicking through their cards to see if there were any deathplace motels; none found, although surely?) and eating as much highway food as they could manage. It was a carefree trip; they had a good amount of money in the bank account from the sale of the red house, prospects ahead, and they still loved each other.

─╱┃╲─

Jarrold parked the van a block up from the café, wanting to see it for the first time on foot. You captured more of the mood that way. The beach was in the other direction, and that's where the kids wanted to go; Gloria told them wait, wait until we're sorted. They'd check into a motel soon, and then the apparent holiday could begin.

—⁄⁀⁀—

The family peered in through dusty windows. It was pretty on the outside, clearly an older building, and inside, already, Gloria and Joy saw features that delighted them.

"You thinking of buying the place?" An old man, neatly dressed but with stains on his coat lapel, bald patches in his beard, a sideways tilt, asked Jarrold. "Needs a bit of sprucing up but I tell ya, the locals will be in your debt, sir." He tugged his forelock then exccuted an elaborate bow.

"Thinking about it." Jarrold didn't confess they had no idea how to run a café, nor that they had already bought it.

"There's a safe in the cellar no one's been able to crack if you need any further enticement. That'll be all yours."

There was a neat little apartment up top too, which Joy was already negotiating for.

"Why don't you buy the place? A few of you club together and get it?" Jarrold asked the old man. He often asked a real estate agent this question. If you were good at reading people you soon got to the heart of the matter.

"Us? No. We'd drink up the profits in no time flat. That last lot . . . " the old man shuddered. "You heard about the murder?"

"The chefs? Diddling each other and the husband shot them? Yeah. But that was a long time ago. Ay? Out of living memory."

"Oh, that one. Yeah, long gone, who cares. Nah, this one happened a couple of years ago. Gruesome story. Gruesome!"

"I love a bit of blood and guts," Jarrold said, although he was squeamish and blood-averse.

"The owners went on holiday, we thought. Nice couple they were, those modern types with fancy clothes, that sort of hair, you know." He rubbed at his own grey, wiry hair. "They didn't put a sign up or anything, that would have been asking for trouble! But someone figured it out, anyway. A local bloke broke into the place, smashed a window round the back where no one could see, and crept through the kitchen to get to the cash register. Or we all reckon he woulda just stole the booze and the cigarettes. But something went wrong. No one knows if it was murder or an accident."

The old man paused, peering impishly at Jarrold, who performed as directed.

"Why's that?" he asked.

"They didn't find Davey's body until the owners got back. By which stage, awful. Hot weather. Flies got in through the smashed window. It was like a carpet of a person. A carpet," the old man said, spreading his fingers out as if running them through shag pile. "Once it was all cleaned up, the owners decided to start the early opening. Because he only broke in for the booze, you know? They figured if they opened early, no one would have to break in. Yeah, yeah, logics. But it worked for all of us. He was an alcoholic from way back. That guy. Sad bloody life he had; his mother disappeared when he was two and he was in and out of foster care. Lost himself in booze to forget about how bad it was, how angry he was."

Davey was 46, the old man said, just celebrated a birthday by smashing up a couple dozen headstones at the cemetery. "Looking for his mum," the old man said, shaking his head.

―∕∣∖―

The whole family stripped off the old ruined wallpaper and cleaned the walls with sugar soap to get out the stink of cigarette smoke and grease. The old man ("Call me George, everyone does") helped out, providing the scrubbing brushes and finding buckets.

"Do you have a vision?" the old man said. "They used to have hundreds of photos up. They had the Prime Minister in here once! And a bloke who pretended to be Charlie Chaplin, did such a good job no one knew the difference. And Errol Flynn, too."

They found the pile of photos themselves and flicked through them, curling edges, yellowed with smoke, graffitied. D.H. Lawrence was there, with 'Who?' scrawled across him. No one wanted to put those back up again.

There were newspaper clippings, faded by the sun and fly-spotted. Any time the café or the town made it into the news.

Gloria suggested the cigarette cards of her father's collection, and they all spent a day sorting them and laying them out. There were many thousands.

"Is this crazy?" Gloria asked.

Joy wanted something out of a fashion magazine. She waved it around. But the others all helped to cover the walls with cards, even the Deathplace set, which looked well at home amongst the Modern Wonders, Prominent Golfers, Bridges of West Country, Film Stars with their Pets, Holiday Resorts.

Over time, the customers would stick their own cards up, adding to the collection.

"These bloody things multiply," Jarrold said, but they already knew that.

-,⟋⟍-

The kitchen was disgusting and had to be completely gutted, every single bit removed, floor replaced, wall coverings.

On their first day of opening, Gloria heard voices just after 6am. They were all sleeping in the flat upstairs, apart from Joy, who'd decided on the granny flat. They were excited by their opening day, wanting everything to be perfect.

Gloria padded downstairs in her nightie. The café was filled with flitting shadows as the sun rose and a trick of the light meant it looked like people were sitting in the booths. Another trick showed people outside peeking in, and she squealed as she realized there really were people out there. She raced upstairs to dress, then down again without waking Jarrold, tying on an apron, brushing her hair with her palms.

There were three of them out there. She shook her head, pointing at the 'Closed' sign, but one of them gestured to his watch.

"Early opener," he called. He was a piggy little man who did, in fact, run pigs. Rumor had already told her the town joke—that if you had a body to dispose of, he was your man. "It was always an early opener," the pig farmer said, stepping inside. The other two men entered as well, shoulders curved, heads bowed, as if ashamed.

It was all an act, she quickly realized as she poured them a beer. She wondered why they didn't drink at home. She really didn't mind, although Jarrold wasn't keen on customers who liked to drink that early.

"They're shift workers," she said, although she had no idea. The liquor license came with the place; why not use it? Gloria could never sleep, anyway, struggling through to three or four in the morning, then giving up and getting out of bed. If she liked reading it'd be okay. She could lie in bed lost in another world. But she hated reading.

Gloria loved serving at the bar, all the flirting, the jokes, the progression of loudness. She served drinks as long as people kept paying. She set up a series of lamps on the bar, and in their soft pink glow she felt like an angel or something.

"Isn't she a stunner?" one of the men called out to Jarrold. "Younger by the minute."

"She bathes in the blood of her victims, that's why. We call her Countess Bathory."

The man laughed. He repeated the comment to the others at this table, all of them sitting around like great philosophers. They'd been gathering here and elsewhere for decades, sitting like this, talking like this. Men like this gathered in multinational coffee shops in the city, sitting on small stools, ignoring their surroundings, imagining they were still in Greece or Italy or anywhere but there. Jarrold liked to sit with the old men out the front. He liked to hear them talk; they were not afraid of philosophy, or opinions. They believed in ghosts and retribution and at least one of them had taken a life.

Jarrold wondered what it was like to take a life. He had been in many deathplaces and yet he had never felt the urge to create his own.

━╱╿╲━

The café was an easy business. Hard work but not stressful, most of the time. Jarrold insisted on paying the children (although he also stopped buying them 'extras') and they all worked hard. Joy wasn't interested in serving customers or cleaning, but she didn't mind cooking, and Sunday became known as Joy Day, when Joy would create snacks and sweets. She'd already decided she didn't want to finish school, a place she considered tedious and pointless.

Living so close to a surf beach meant an entire change of lifestyle for the children. The boys and Joy became surfies, their hair blonding, their skin tanned, their confidence on the waves growing by the day. In exchange for stolen beers from the café the locals let them learn, helped them out, welcomed them in.

━╱╿╲━

Rhiannon became an obsessive shell collector. She could only go to the beach if an older person took her, something she found terribly unfair. If no one would take her, sometimes she'd sneak out and stomp off by herself. She knew the way. It was one road, then turn to your writing hand when you saw the purple house. Joy had taught her that, saying that no matter what, you have to know where you are.

27

Leeanne? Went with the flow.

Jarrold enjoyed it as much as Gloria did, and he liked to be generous, giving things away to needy people and others as well. They even managed to open the safe, Jarrold putting all his weight behind the drill, Gloria and Joy levering the door, Martin and Maurice tipping the whole thing slightly forward. Inside they found a good amount of money, some naked photos Gloria quickly tucked away, two watches, a pearl necklace, some papers regarding ownership and value of the coach out the back that made Jarrold happy, and an envelope with *'davey's things'* written on it. Inside that, a photo of a dead man, lying on the café floor. A tiny knitted doll. A wallet, empty except for a note that said *'For my Davey boy from Mummy'*. And a rusty spoon.

➤⟋⟨⟍➤

It was a Sunday evening. Joy was cooking. The boys were pretending to do homework. Leeanne did hers carefully. It was an assignment about the Olympic Games, and she painstakingly cut out circles with a pair of nail scissors, then colored them in. They had found boxes of pens and color pencils and felt-tip pens when they moved in.

Gloria said, "If you color them first, you don't have to stay in the lines. You can cut off the outside bits."

Rhiannon moved restlessly from table to table. She was bored by Leeanne who, disagreeing with her mother's tip, was slowly coloring in the Olympic rings, already cut and moving around.

The boys wouldn't let her see what they were doing, so it must be rude.

Joy sat her up on a stool and got her to shell peas.

There were a few customers. Two from out of town, on their way somewhere. A table of young people, sunburnt and sandy, trying to order booze with a bad fake ID. And a woman on her own, wearing a sundress that was too tight and very revealing. Jarrold made her a salad sandwich on request, and a chocolate milkshake, and she asked what the house specialty was.

Joy called out "Mango Muffins today," but the woman shook her head, disgusted. Jarrold moved around the café, clearing tables, chatting, being charming. He was still fit and handsome, everyone said.

It wasn't until later, after the boys disappeared, that he became flaccid and disgusting.

The woman stared at the Deathplace cards. "Are they for sale?" "Over my dead body," Jarrold thundered. "No, truly. The kids can sell them when I die, but until then I'm hanging on to them. They help me figure out what's going to happen next."

"Can you tell me?"

"Is there anything in particular you want to know about?"

"I want to know . . . am I kidding myself about being an artist? Am I actually talented or deluded? Will I ever sell a painting or win a prize?"

Jarrold nodded. "Are there any cards you feel particularly connected to? Anything at all?"

Rhiannon watched closely. Others all gathered around, loving it, loving the joke. The woman picked Railway Station, Bridge and Café. Jarrold shook his head sorrowfully. The woman ordered a bottle of wine.

"Is it bad?" she said.

"The good news is, the fact that you're asking about your innate talent means you must have it," Jarrold said. He pulled the three cards carefully off the wall, turning them over and over. He asked her to describe what she saw.

"The railway station is pretty rundown, so why is there someone standing on the platform? He has a suitcase which looks really old and he seems sad. I can't read the name of the station but there is smoke in the distance. I'm not sure if it's a train approaching or that's from a chimney in a house."

Jarrold nodded. "Go on."

"The Bridge one looks quite scary but I think it means a crossing over to the other side, like making a choice that will change your life." She squinted closely at the card. "I think there are faces in the water. Or there is like a treasure chest under there, right at the bottom, so if you dived in from the bridge you could grab it."

"And this one?" He pushed the Café Card towards her.

Gloria stood behind him now, her hand on his shoulder. He'd never done this sort of reading before. Never played with a customer like this. She studied the woman; she was attractive in a self-indulged kind of a way. She'd be tanned all over, Gloria was sure. She squeezed Jarrold's shoulder and he patted her hand.

"It's this café, isn't it?" the woman said. "Definitely. It looks almost the same except you've fixed it up a bit. There's a man there, in one of the booths, but it's empty apart from that. I wonder if he was one of the owners or something. Or just a lonely man."

The boys exchanged glances, shaking their heads. Neither of them had seen that man in the card before.

Jarrold cleared his throat. He was disturbed, also, but they knew the cards changed. This one in particular was fluid. "So," he said. "You've chosen these three because they gave you a positive sense. Of a good future, but also of loneliness, but as an artist you would often work alone. That sense of solitude is important to your creativity."

She nodded vigorously. Her pupils dilated and she swung her leg under the table, tapping Jarrold's knee *tap tap tap tap tap*.

He said, "You've chosen these cards with a purpose, rather than a feeling, which means that you might be surprised by what you hear." He gave a short smile, and in that moment something flickered over his face, something cruel and unfamiliar. "The railway station represents a journey, of course. Some journeys are to a better place. Some are short trips before we return to what we know. And some mean we cannot retrace our steps, that each furlong the train travels takes us further from the familiar. For you, the familiar is the talent you've been told all your life you have."

No one stopped him because they had not heard him be cruel. They didn't expect they would need to stop him.

"Your talent has been leaving you for months now. It's the encroachment of age, of boredom and staidness. The disappearing of ideas."

The woman gasped.

"The Bridge stands over treasure indeed, but in your case it is treasure that will not be discovered until you are dead. Do you have artworks stashed away? Finished or unfinished?"

She nodded.

"That will be the treasure discovered when you are dead. Representations of your work when your talent was natural."

Joy laughed, a shocked kind of laugh.

"And this café? That man?" Jarrold held the card up and sniffed it. "This card represents the afterlife, and this man is the one who will send you there. Study him close. He's the one who'll end your life."

"When?" We had to lean close to hear her. "Who is it?"

"That I can't say. Make the most of each day, is all I can say."

In the card, there was a man, sitting in one of the booths, a beer in front of him. His shoulders were slumped but his face was tilted up so they could see it clearly, see the features.

"Looks like our Davey," Old George said.

Later, it was Rhiannon who scrabbled through the old news clippings and found the one about Davey, who'd died on their floor and now, it seemed, featured in the card.

Joy offered her a cold collation. She said, "It was the King of Denmark's favorite meal," and put a high price tag on it.

It was just a plate of cheese and ham with some pickles; over time it proved to be one of their best sellers. She couldn't get the pickle jar open so her dad made a performance of opening it. There wasn't a jar he couldn't open; it said so on the blackboard menu. It was a sad little party trick but one that made them all laugh. And customers brought in jars with lids so tight they hadn't been opened for years and *zip zip* they were done.

Martin did it, too. "Pretty strong for a little man," the woman said.

"Fuck off, ugly," Martin said.

Maurice said, "Dad won't sell that set but we've got a lot of them if you want one. Like the Wrinkled Cow set."

Martin laughed. They could always rely on each other for support. "There's the Women of Genius," and he made his fingers do air quotes.

The woman looked confused.

"My favourite is Fashion Disasters," Joy said. "Or Unappreciated Food Items."

The woman's eyes opened at this.

"Famous Café Receipts," Gloria said, to hide their teasing.

"Long Shopping Dockets," Jarrold said.

They all started talking over each other, wanting to come up with the funniest one.

"Very Large Tips on Patterned Plates."

"Rocks of the town of Geelong."

The sillier and more obscure the better. The woman customer had long since lost interest; the man who owned the surf shop came in, and they were now huddled together in a booth, laughing and ignoring the rest of the world. It started to pour outside, and suddenly the place was filled with people seeking shelter and drinks, a buzz of excitement in the air.

At one stage Joy said, "It was hard to tell the men from the pigs," quoting *Animal Farm* which they'd read at school (the only bit of school work she'd enjoyed all year) and Gloria murmured her agreement. It was hard to tell who was real in the café and who was a shadow. Martin in particular loved it, flitting about from table to table, breathing in as if absorbing the scents and the experience of everybody in there.

Men sat at the bar. Old George, who was always there, who didn't seem to have a home to go to, loved his top corner where he could watch the comings and goings, hear the gossip, make his opinions known. He ordered two beers. He sometimes did that, saying he was buying one for a dead friend. He set the two of them up in front of him, drank one, left the other. Ordered another. Sometimes he left the second beer all night, other times he'd forget and drink it.

This time, lights flickered in a momentary power failure, and he jumped up as if someone poked him. The beer went flying, most of it on the floor but half of it on the drinker sitting next to him quietly sinking into his whiskey.

"You evil fucken' bastard," the whiskey drinker said, but George bought him another real quick and they both settled. George was spooked, though, looking over his shoulder, jumping at shadows.

—/\〉—

Later that night, once all the drinkers had gone (one of the regulars climbing into the old coach and sleeping there) and the family were upstairs settled into their beds, Gloria was filled with restlessness. There was a smell in the air that excited her, a smell like ozone, or oranges, or something like that. She went downstairs to look out onto the street. If she did it in the dark, sometimes she could watch lovers fighting or kissing, she could see wandering animals, or she could see someone curled up in the gutter, sleeping the sleep of the righteous.

This time, instead, she found Martin spread-eagled on the floor, stretched out as far as he could reach.

"What are you doing?" she whispered, not wanting to wake him if he was sleep walking.

He shifted and stretched more, one eye opening to look at her. "This is where the long-dead man lay," he said. "On this very spot."

And she was sure she heard whistling, not of the wind but of a jaunty man. Outside they seemed to gather until she focused, and the sight of her son playing dead made her feel sick to her stomach.

➤⟋⟍➤

For all that, looking back, the café years were easily the best. They worked hard, but they stayed put. And while the café was full of atmosphere and stains, ghosts and the dregs of ghosts, somehow they were all settled too—perhaps grateful, even, to be amongst people who understood. It was, looking back, the eye of the storm. The peaceful and ordinary time before.

You've got to destroy before you can improve.

CARD 22/24
SHOPPING CENTRE COURTYARD, COOLANGATTA, QLD

Built in the 1960s, this shopping center is a perfect example of brutalist architecture produced by replication rather than inspiration. Intended as a social hub, the shops sit around a square, with the supermarket on one side, and a bottle shop, a bakery and a butcher on the other sides. In the courtyard itself, concrete seats and tables sit, visible cracks showing within months of installation, never to be replaced.

On the cement squares that were once a deliberate range of colors but are now all an uncomfortable grey, at least four patches of blood are visible. There have been more, but these are the most recent.

They all hated going to the supermarket for supplies. Dad was pissed off they'd run out of the mass-supply stuff (mince for hamburgers, frozen chips, lettuce) so he wouldn't even be grateful. And you couldn't go to the small local shop because that was too bloody expensive, so you had to walk twenty minutes down to the big supermarket (or get a lift if someone was offering—but they all knew what happened to hitchhikers). Everyone knew the butchers was a drug front, that an order of extra sausage was actually an order for weed, and ground beef (as opposed to mince, which was mince) was an order for speed. That's why the junkies clustered like burrs on socks in the open area, setting up makeshift seats of milk crates or whatever they could find. They'd scavenge for enough coins to buy a single bottle of beer from the booze shop, downing it in one go before reaching the others so they wouldn't have to share.

Joy made Martin buy her 'sausage' for her; she was too well known, she said. She offered to pay him, or to let him come along to the next party she went to, and he agreed. He dragged Maurice along for the company, but when the boys didn't return within the hour, Leeanne and Rhiannon were sent by Joy, who was the one tasked with the job in the first place. Leeanne had begged for the responsibility; at twelve she was still treated like a baby, she said. It was just on dusk. If Gloria had been home (she was out at her sewing club) she would have gone herself. Jarrold didn't really notice.

Leeanne took the opportunity to complain about the embarrassment of all of this. She liked that they were buying the things further away, so that their so-called 'secret ingredients' weren't discovered. For the burgers? Pre-prepared with so much added salt. And they didn't cut their own potatoes for chips. Shop chips were cheaper, but they charged for 'hand cut'. She hated it when the customers ordered 'home chips', identical but a dollar more. Maybe a shake of chicken salt, or dried parsley. She hated lying to her friends.

She didn't have many friends.

―﹍﹍―

The lights in the courtyard were that bluish color so the veins wouldn't show and people couldn't inject drugs. It didn't stop them hanging around, though. Rhiannon held onto Leeanne's jeans, not wanting to look closely at the people milling around. Were they people? Some of them looked like the shadows in the café sometimes when she snuck down to steal a bit of cake or something while everyone was asleep.

"Hey, look. Sweet meat," a man said. He was enormous—twice the size of their father—but gaunt, his clothes hanging off him, his face so long Rhiannon thought it had been stretched. Leeanne tugged Rhiannon to run but they were surrounded suddenly, the smell of old dust thick in the air.

"Leave them." It was a much smaller man, shoes falling off his feet, clothing dark and damaged. His eyes were a bright, clear blue, even in the failing light, and he said, "Girls, call your dad to come get you."

They ran to a phone box and called for their father, who shouted furiously at Joy before slamming down the phone. He was there in minutes, stalking through the people and the ghosts, the latter clinging to him like maggots, like ticks, as he arrived, his apron still on, dirty from the café.

➤⟋⟍➤

A new card appeared on the wall. The shopping center courtyard. Empty apart from two small figures, which they thought at first were the girls but were, in fact, Martin and Maurice.

After the boys disappeared, all of us changed. Joy couldn't bear facing any sort of reality and was much happier drunk. She insisted on keeping the café open late, covering the bar and all of it, which was good for business but not for her peace of mind.

Mum refused to look at any of the customers. She was sure one of these men took the boys.

Mum and Dad visited Deathplaces to calm themselves. They said they were looking for the boys, but why would the boys be at a country pub, ·or the mall, or the river, or an island?

We stayed behind. We never closed the café. We just had *party party party*.

CARD 13/24
THE EAGLE, NSW

Built in 1950, this pub is a direct facsimile of the Eagle in Cambridge, England. From the appearance of two buildings crammed together, to the attic, to the large bay window on one side, the architect took great care to replicate every detail. There are names scrawled on the ceiling in the main bar, many more hundreds now than when the pub was built.

In this pub, it is tradition to buy two beers at a time. One for yourself, and one for the dead, who get very thirsty. In 1952, an apparent accidental poisoning led to the deaths of twelve pub goers, an event which surprisingly didn't close the place down.

In this pub, alongside the bottles of rarely-drunk brandy and scotch, jars line up filled with dirt. It's said that each jar contains the dirt from the grave of a man who died in this place. Whether or not this is true, it certainly acts as a drawcard for the more morbid among drinkers.

CARD 21/24
THE MOSAIC MALL

This large suburban mall was opened in 1971 and has resisted an upgrade ever since. These days the quirks of '70s styling are considered charming, but for many years the era was seen as ugly and lacking in creativity. At three floors it is a modest mall, but most shoppers would find all they need amongst the businesses here. It almost closed the same year it opened, with the tragic death of an elderly lady in a random act of violence. She was stabbed as she headed toward the bakery for the cinnamon buns she so adored.

He stabbed her three times fast in the chest. She felt it, but was so used to aches and pains she thought her heart was twinging as it was prone to do. The man who'd bumped into her didn't stop to help, and no one else noticed, so she made her way to a seat to recover. Hand to chest is when she noticed the blood. Most of it soaked up into her woolen clothing, and she was too astonished and then too weak to ask for help. She didn't even get her buns.

A plaque bearing the old lady's name was added some time in the '80s, by a relative perhaps, or center management. The seat itself had never been upgraded and was barely used. Rumor said that if her seat was removed she would haunt the mall, and no one wanted to be responsible for that. It was tested out in the early '90s, when an enthusiastic manager decided the shopping *center should be modernized, to attract teenagers who'd come and spend their money. In the refurbishment, the old lady's seat was shoved down into the basement. If there wasn't a rise in violent incidents, accidents and arguments, you couldn't tell staff and customers so. There was such an outcry the seat was returned to its position, carefully painted, with the plaque shiny and readable. Things quietened down in the shopping center after that.*

CARD 10/24
MEMORIAL PARK, MURRAY RIVER, VICTORIA

If you time lapse the last few hundred years, the banks of most rivers would be strewn with bodies. This park, modelled on the memorial gardens, Stratford-Upon-Avon, is peaceful and idyllic, the perfect place for a pleasant picnic. Like the original gardens, this park has the church spire in the distance.

This card commemorates one loss of life in particular—that of a local gravedigger, erroneously accused of burying a lost child beneath an official interment. The child was found hours later, playing with newborn kittens in a neighbor's shed, but by then the gravedigger was drowned, head held under by the grief-stricken father seeking answers. All pleas of temporary insanity aside, that father was imprisoned, and murdered in jail, so we remember another death with this card.

CARD 6/24
AN ISLAND COVERED WITH RARE FLOWERS

They call it Wild Island and you never go there alone. The number of bones out there is uncountable, although habit and tradition say you line up bones if you find them and this will stave off the ghosts.

Pan lives here, they say, in this island wilderness. Certainly the deaths, the so-called sacrifices, that still occur to this day are performed in his honor. The death commemorated on this card happened in 1912 and caused a great sensation at the time. The heir apparent slashed the throat of the heir presumptive to a large family business. The death was particularly gruesome and captured, frame by frame, by the bevy of young women also camped out on the island.

My brothers" bodies were found in the sand dunes, and alongside them, close by, syringes and aluminum foil.

'Teens Overdose in Dunes.'

We knew they didn't die here, though. There they were, on Card 22, the courtyard. That's where they died. So who moved them?

CARD 24/24
SEMI-DETACHED, CANBERRA

Built in the early 1970s by a developer who fancied themselves memorable, these five semi-detached houses (one of which is depicted) stood on the approach to the main shopping center. Orange brick with a lower layer of render (also orange), these two-story residences shared a wall. Large street-side windows look into the small loungeroom, rarely used by residents beyond the storage of furniture due to the lack of privacy during the day. Even thick curtains don't keep out the car headlights as they turn. A small kitchen with a built-in breakfast bar and a toilet that is effectively outside make up the ground floor, while upstairs three small bedrooms of similar size and an inordinately large, brown-tiled bathroom complete the rooms. The laundry is outside.

The bedrooms being the same size, the on-street location, and the ugly décor make these houses perfect for groups of students.

They would be knocked down in 2015, with no evidence of them left whatsoever. Even knowing that deaths occurred here, we see no trace. A suicide by hanging; a fall in the bath by a lonely man who hadn't exactly realized that no one cared; the poisoning of a boyfriend; the stabbing of a mother of three by her violent, charming ex-husband. She died protecting her children, and while he didn't physically hurt them, he did leave them alone with her dead body for hours, causing them deep and abiding trauma. The

neighbors heard nothing; he'd been quiet and so had she, and the traffic was always loud.
This is the last card made by the originating painter whose name is long since forgotten. He captured souls in these cards. Vandalized lives.
Enjoy.

Jarrold and Gloria came back from their travels. He looked bad. Overweight in a stuffed-cushion way, like old horsehair shoved in a too-small cover, spikey bits poking out. His flesh was soft and pale and greenish in places, and he had dark, furry patches on him.

Gloria hated the café now; despised the bar. She was still sure one of the men had killed the boys (it wasn't a drug overdose, that much they knew) and she would sit there, staring. Jarrold sat on a chair in the corner like one of the old European men, fat belly meaning he couldn't sit with his knees together even if he wanted to. He wasn't always like this. As a young man he was lithe and small.

He just needed to rest a hand on Gloria's shoulder and she crumpled.

No one stole from the café any more.

—✦—

Gloria negotiated the purchase of the semi-detached house in Canberra. Jarrold was past talking to people, although he imagined he was still charming and attractive. There are people like this, who haven't caught up with the fact they are no longer good-looking, that people no longer find them charismatic. The language is still there, and the body language, but the charisma is gone.

Both of them upstairs, tearing at the carpet, scratching at the floorboards, and the three girls helping, exchanging glances but letting it be.

—✦—

They made a good deal of money selling their renovated café, enough to buy both sides of these semi-detached houses. Both sides had fallen into disrepair, with tenants claiming strange noises, awful stains appearing out of nowhere, black mold and other reasons to skip out early on the lease and not respect the property.

They moved into one side while renovating the other, with Joy getting her own room (under threat of moving out, which really it was time she did), Leeanne and Rhiannon having to share.

"I hate this house," Leeanne said.

Jarrold was large now, and he oozed a strange thick sweat. Gloria was the opposite, thinner and sweeter by the day it seemed, so that even a quick trip to the shops drew interest and delight. Joy, in usual teenage behavior, dressed as differently as she could, in black and torn clothing. She told anyone who'd listen that she was a foundling, or a changeling, words she didn't really understand but that meant, she thought, that she was not really a member of her own family.

Rhiannon hated it too, but Joy was happy; she'd met a boy, one she really liked, and he was close by. After three or four months, she invited him to meet the family, , as a test. She tried to scare him with stories of murder.

"This is the room it happened in," she said, showing him the small attached glasshouse.

"I can feel it!" the boyfriend said. "I knew something was wrong with this room."

Joy snorted. He'd failed the test. The glasshouse was an extension, so there wasn't even a chance of the dying person dragging themselves through it.

Things don't always end perfectly, in a neat circle, making sense, so you nod your head and say, "Ahhh!"

CARD 17/24
A HIGH SCHOOL BATHROOM

Once the shining star of a government determined to provide free, excellent education for all, this high school has seen better days. Increasingly overlooked by parents, it is mostly local students who go here now, and in small numbers. The teaching staff lack motivation. The school itself is classically ugly in the brutalist sense; grey brick, an occasional attempt at a flourish that failed at the time and is now an eyesore, windows not washed in many years, and bathrooms that—while apparently renovated over the decades—should more be described as plastered over.

The death that occurred here was as tragic and as bloody as any seen. It was the janitor who took the girls one after another, like the opposite of the catcher in the rye, slitting their throats and piling them up in the corner store, skirts lifted, underwear removed. When they found him, he said he was just cleaning up.

The floor has been retiled since then, and the walls painted, and the fixtures replaced. The ghost stories are all that remain.

Just as Jarrold chose a preschool because of death, so he chose the high school. They didn't think Leeanne or Rhiannon would be great academics (they'd already accepted Joy wouldn't be); it didn't matter.

On her second week at school, Rhiannon stole the cards. While all of them knew what the circumstance was (that their parents were determined to visit every card in the pack), Rhiannon wanted to see for herself.

She stood in the bathroom, cards in hand. There was little similarity between the card and reality, but the shape of the room was the same. There was someone in the last stall, and Rhiannon knew enough to understand how weird it would be to wait. Then the toilet flushed and a girl came out. She wasn't one of the mean girls, luckily; more one of the ignored, the ones no one else noticed. She looked ashamed as she washed her hands.

"What's that?" this girl said.

Rhiannon showed her the cards, reading them like tarot cards. As she spoke, other girls gathered, and she made her descriptions as gruesome as possible. When she read about the murdered girls in this bathroom, she understood almost straight away that she'd gone too far. Terrifying people was not a good idea if you wanted to make friends.

But the girls remained fascinated, and they determined to all sneak back after school, turn the lights out, and have a séance.

That night, Rhiannon told her family she was studying at a friend's house. Her parents were out (visiting a deathplace, perhaps; they didn't always confess) and Joy had her boyfriend over, taking advantage of the almost empty house. Leeanne asked if she could come, and Rhiannon told her to read a book instead.

➤ ⁄ ❘ ＼ ◄

"Where did these cards come from?" one of the girls asked. They'd easily snuck in through a window and there was no alarm in this crappy school. They could do whatever they wanted, but all they wanted to do was have a séance.

"My mum got them from my grandad; I don't know where he got them from. But did you know that a dead man held onto them for a long time? If you sniff hard you can smell the dead body."

One of the girls was game enough; it made her dry retch into the bathroom sink.

"Was it your brothers?" another girl whispered.

They all knew about her brothers. She showed them the card with them in it, visible if you squinted close enough. Then she had them sit in a circle. One of the girls had stolen a tiny bottle of brandy from her parents' liquor cabinet, enough for a sip each. And Rhiannon had searched under Joy's bed for the leftover bottles she threw there. There was always a bit in those.

Rhiannon sat cross-legged. She was making this up as she went along, with the brandy giving her confidence. Moonlight shone through the window they'd all climbed in through, and Rhiannon had brought along a scented candle. It didn't quite cover the wet cement/past shit smell of the room, but it helped. She placed the 24 cards out face down, without looking at them. Some of the edges were slightly singed, some felt furry to the touch. The backs of the cards carried the story of the front, and some of the girls strained to read the tiny writing.

Rhiannon waved her hands over the cards. She said, "Girls girls girls who are dead. Girls who are alive want to talk to you. If you are here, move your cards."

The cards didn't move, but there was a shuffling sound, a whispering, from one of the stalls. The girls squealed.

Rhiannon leant over and pushed the door open. "Are you in there? Is there anything left of you? Is there a sign?"

She told the girls her father believed something was always left behind. A small symbol, a scratch in the wall, a chip in the tile. There was plenty of that in this poorly maintained bathroom.

Rhiannon flipped over card 17, the high school bathroom, and she said, "Look closely. Can you see them? Maybe in the mirror?" Silently, breath held, they all looked.

"Can you feel your throats? Sore? Mine is. I can't even swallow. I can't," Rhiannon said, and she wasn't even lying, she felt like a knife was drawn across her throat and she could feel warmth there, as if her blood was spilling. She gathered the cards, her breath shallow.

One of the girls coughed, spluttered, *I can't breathe*, and the others too, then all of them in a panic out the window and running to the gate. Once there, they hugged each other.

"If we stick together we'll be okay," Rhiannon said, but already they'd moved away from her, wanting distance, and she'd lost them.

Ghosts caught around his ankles like barbed wire.

CARD 1/24
PINEAPPLE FARM, SUNSHINE COAST, QUEENSLAND

Did you know pineapples grow low, from bushes, rather than high, like coconuts? It isn't a true fruit. It's a thoroughly resilient plant, grown from fusion of spikes of flowers to create 'a perfumed juicy mass'.

This card shows beautifully ripe pineapples, and majestic, colorful mountains in the background, a bit misty. Sturdy looking farmhouses in between. A worker bends over, cutting fruit with a large knife, while another carries a full basket away along a well-worn path. On these fields, tensions and passions can run high amongst workers. Those large machetes for cutting pineapples off the stalk provide temptation, and remove the need for a moment's thought, and this is how, in 1870, a young man from Sydney lost his head. He was found days later when the plantation owners did a rare inspection.

The original painter was just 18 when he created this card. His family motto was 'always remember, never forgive' although there is no recorded reason as to why.

Joy refused to travel with them on this working holiday, preferring to continue working in the bar where she would be manager within a couple of months.

Jarrold and Gloria would have liked a third driver for this thirteen-hour trip, but managed fine without her. Rhiannon and Leeanne shared the backseat, a stack of pillows and snacks between them. Leeanne remained dreamy and disconnected, annoying Rhiannon by being so boring.

"I was almost killed by a car," Jarrold said into the silence. "I was in one of the worst bus accidents the country has ever seen."

Gloria looked at him, smiling. This was actually her story; he'd forgotten.

"I was the only survivor. They had to cut me loose. They lined all the bodies up in the aisle of a church and they didn't even tell anyone they were doing it. All those poor churchgoers arriving the next day thought they'd died themselves and gone to hell."

Jarrold had a lot of stories about beating death.

━╱╿╲━

They stayed in caravans at the pineapple farm and worked hard all day. Rhiannon loved it, although she was only given a small, quite useless knife to cut the pineapples.

That part of our holiday had to be cut short when Leeanne had an extended allergic reaction to the bromelain in the pineapple. Joy said over the phone that the pineapple was eating her alive, which made Leeanne cry. It tingled the mouth of the others; Leeanne felt as if she was disappearing.

> They only cared about cards, were completely driven by them. It's not a holiday at all; it was another deathplace.

CARD 12/24
BEACH APARTMENT IN A BUILT-UP BLOCK

Overlooking the ocean, this 17th floor apartment is recently repainted. Residents can no longer stand on the miniscule balcony, and none of the windows open, following a number of suicides all from this apartment. The view of the ocean and the jagged rocks made this the apartment of choice.

There are no hand marks or other obvious indications this is the spot. Before the windows were nailed shut, people would throw down whole watermelons to see them smash, something quite triggering for the witnesses of one or more suicides.

➤➤ ｜ ◄◄

'What I Did on the Holidays' by Rhiannon Carstairs

Our apartment overlooked the beach and was on the top floor. Dad said it was the best view. There was a small balcony but you couldn't get on it because the door was welded shut! Because so many people killed themselves. The hotel people left a table and chair out there and there was someone's ashtray full of butts.

Leeanne said she was tired and went to bed. Dad and I went to the beach but I was nervous about the undertow and how high the waves were. Dad got out amongst it!!

I found a thick gold chain down the back of the couch. Yes it is probably fake but I still like it. It's hard to say who it belonged to. My dad gave us a lecture about someone called the Venerable Bead, who died with nothing. He gave away even the small things in his pockets. And there were men who got burnt to death who did the same thing. One of them gave away a handkerchief. Dad said they thought that ownership at death meant you were trapped by your belongings. He said this gold chain must have been left by someone who died and at least they weren't trapped. Six people chucked themselves off the balcony last year. It's the view of the ocean and down below (once it's done once there's a mood, right? A feeling? And others will do it). There's no sign of it but Dad looked, of course. He's peering through the sealed glass door, thinking about smashing it. Trying to find a sign. In my room, he found out someone had OD'd in there. I guess people do it in hotel rooms so they are found in a day or so? He pulled the bed away from the wall and cut away a tiny bit of carpet tile.

After fish and chips on Sunday I went down to the beach to get a suntan (don't laugh; I know I'm white as a ghost) but I didn't go down the beach. I've had this nightmare, and I woke up with a woman lying next to me, pressed up close, crying open-mouthed, her teeth half broken away, and I hit the light but she was gone.

So I searched around down in the carpark. I moved rubbish bins, looked behind the walls. Then I lifted a big plant pot, kind of rolled it out of the way, and underneath were bugs and two busted teeth. I smashed that plant pot to move it. "You rotten little vandal," someone called me.

Anyway my sister Leeanne was eaten alive by bromelain and disappeared but she didn't feel a thing.

Teacher's comment: *You were supposed to write a true story.*

My comment: *I did. Leeanne is gone.*

CARD 8/24
HIKER'S HUT, VICTORIA

Made of stone and wood, this hut was built in honour of a man who died on the mountain. It is a single room, with a toilet outside, a rainwater sink, and fold down wooden beds. It is considered haunted by most hikers who have stayed the night. A fireplace dominates the room alongside a high pile of firewood and a sign asking people to replace it.

This card commemorates an elaborate murder which took place here in 1931. It remained unsolved until 1972, when the drop toilet was replaced with a composting system and the murder weapon (a small axe) was found. Scratched into the handle were the words "I did it" and initials, a seeming scream for help that led to the arrest of an elderly man who accepted incarceration with apparent relief.

Jarrold and Gloria have not been apart for any length of time since the day they met at the pub. He tried not to think of her as he marched through the trees, over hills, crossed rivers. He had lied to the girls, said he was just going walking, no destination in mind.

There was always a destination in mind.

He sometimes felt as if he controlled the ghosts, sometimes as if the ghosts controlled him. Mostly he didn't believe in them; it was the memories, that was all. The trauma of death, the fury at

life being done. He felt anger when he never felt anger. He felt
regret for his choices and yet he was choosing this again, choosing
to visit yet another deathplace.

━╱╷╲━

He settled his backpack into the corner and stacked wood into the
enclosed fire. There wasn't much there (the last visitor perhaps
ignoring the sign asking them to replace it—that a life might be
saved by a stack of wood here) and so he spent an hour collecting
twigs and larger branches, far more than he needed. The exercise
puffed him out, although for all his size he was still quite fit, no
matter what his doctor told him.

Once the fire was going, he laid out the food he'd brought
along. Tins of stew, of soup, packets of biscuits, some chocolate.
The sounds of the forest settled around him.

He lay on the bed, his head resting on his scrunched-up jacket.
Above him he could see scratches in the rafters, and he wondered
if that was where the rope had been tied, if that was where the man
had died.

There was soap by the sink with a dozen different hairs
embedded.

The fire quickly warmed the small hut. It was a well cleared
chimney so very little smoke stayed inside, but he propped open a
window slightly, not wanting to let the mosquitoes in. He took out
the cards and flicked through them, something which brought him
comfort, like looking through his achievements. The Hiker's Hut
had changed slightly; he could see a shadow of a man in the corner,
becoming clearer as Jarrold focused on him.

"Afternoon," Jarrold said, but the figure didn't answer, and the
smell of death rose off the cards, so strong Jarrold threw them
towards the fire.

The figure lifted its fingers to stretch them. They elongated,
reaching for Jarrold. He had thought he was in control of the
ghosts, and yet this one he could see straight through.

"I'm Jarrold," he said. "Did you die here? Are you the one who
died here?" He sniffed the air, smelling something familiar and yet
not.

The ghost didn't speak, just opened its mouth, then closed,
then open, until Jarrold mimicked it, opening his mouth and
swallowing air until he choked.

In a dream now, Jarrold emptied his pockets, laying the things neatly out on the bed. What instinct drove this he couldn't say; he was grateful to have the chance, though. He spoke to himself as he did it, saying, "Cigarette lighter for Joy, pencil for Rhiannon, wallet for Gloria." Nothing for the boys. He knew they hadn't died of a drug overdose. Nothing for Leeanne and he knew how she'd died, as well.

The ghost waited until he was done, then bent forward and reached its hand into his chest. Jarrold sighed. This was a familiar touch. The ghost sank into him for a bit, snuggled in like a cat settling into a familiar cushion. Jarrold recognized the feeling; he'd thought it was heartburn, or high blood pressure, or something. Almost relieved, finding a reason, but filled with unbearable guilt, Jarrold strung a rope over the metal girder in the hut and tugged on it, hoping it would stay. The ghost left then, and he was overwhelmed with terrible grief ('mourning' is too small a word for the loss of a child) and a sense that he had no control over his actions. He couldn't remember hurting his own children; he knew he would find out in hell if he'd done so. To stop the thoughts, driven to it, he hanged himself. He would swell and discolor and split like a ripe plum.

People said Dad wasn't himself.

As if that excused it.

CARD 14/24
ISOLATED BEACH HOUSE

The beach house sits on the edge of a low cliff. The land around it is sandy. Only succulents grow here, and strange, hardy plants that can live anywhere. The house is single story, surrounded by an enclosed verandah for evenings without mosquitoes and days without flies. The place is solidly built, a transported family home, and decorated by someone with a sure touch, not afraid of greys and vibrant colors. There are no ghosts in this house, no stains or memories left behind of the horrendous murder that took place here in 1958.

Julie Ballard was a young mother of nineteen. Her two-year-old son had multiple health issues after birth complications, and to afford his care (both traditional and alternative medicines) she took clients amongst the men she met. Most of them were fine, perfectly kind to her, and decent lovers. Sometimes, though, they took out all the frustrations and fury on her. She learned to separate herself, to think of time at school (she hadn't been a good student but she was popular and well-liked, not always the same thing) and parties, and her boyfriend, and her son.

Your Uncle Rufus did it, Gloria. Killed her, buried her, kept her secret for decades. Until his deathbed, when he told your father, Gloria. Who unburied her, took what she held, and covered her up again, to save the family name and because he just didn't care.

Jarrold was found six months after his death, by two hikers who thought they'd seen it all. It wasn't a popular hiking route. The rope had rotted through and he had fallen, landing on the cards. He'd been bitten by insects and other small creatures, and the things he'd so carefully laid out were tipped over and lost.

He was not so cruel as to die without identification, and so his remains, and the cards, were returned to his family.

Gloria had never seen the beach house card before.

"One more," Gloria said. "I'll go. You stay here. I have to go."

Rhiannon flicked through the other cards, her nose wrinkling, her fingers feeling sticky and slimy. The Hiker's Hut now pictured a man slumped in the corner. The beach apartment she looked at very closely, seeking Leeanne, and there was perhaps a shadow in the bathroom? Arms stretched out, as if beseeching?

—⟋↑⟍—

The words blurred and changed as Gloria read them.

"What?" Joy said. "What?"

The image on the front of the card had changed too, even as they stood there, and now there was an expanse of dirt in front of the house, with a child's toy sitting there, large and lost. The house itself was long since uninhabitable, left to rot and ruin. They had booked a motel in town and left their things there, hoping not to spend long at this place. They would look for the sort of sign that Jarrold always sought, then consider it done. Even the thought of it gave Gloria a great sense of relief. They'd have a nice dinner, to celebrate working their way through the cards, and they'd talk about things ordinary people talked about.

Holding the card up to compare, they found the patch of dirt. It was covered with weeds now, but the toy was still there: an old truck, rusted and with some sharp edges.

Joy, meanwhile, had called the local police. She said, "We need witnesses. If Grandad and whatever, Granduncle, did some bad shit, we need witnesses."

Rhiannon wanted to dig herself. She loved a mystery. She started, then felt nauseous, dizzy, but also elated. She hadn't had sex yet (not even close) but this, she would eventually discover, is what orgasm felt like.

➤/|\◂

And so the men came and dug up the grave and they found what remained of Julie there, her skeleton hands folded over her stomach as if protecting something, but thank God there was no baby—just this young woman, almost a baby herself. A smell rose up that made all three women exchange glances; the smell of the cards. This is what the cards smelled like.

➤/|\◂

Gloria was tired. She wanted to lie down in the dirt and sleep. The shock of finding out the truth about her beloved (not beloved) father, and the uncle she'd not really known. The loss of her truly beloved Jarrold. Everything had changed.

They vandalized this place, pulled it to bits, tore off bits of wall, smashed the windows. It was already a wreck but they wrecked it further, screaming as they did so, all three of them wild.

Joy put the cards down in the middle of the house, wanting them to burn. They set fire to them using Jarrold's cigarette lighter and watched the pack smolder. A gust of wind blew through the broken windows, lifting the cards, sending them whirling through the air like flying demons, red-edged and with apparent intent. One landed in Gloria's hair; she swept it off with a shout.

Then they all sank, sizzled. None were any more than singed. And Gloria said, "Every one of them is different," and she started to sort them, already planning the visits.

50

"You don't have to, Mum. We can ignore them," Rhiannon said.

"You can. I can't. Thank Uncle Rufus. If I don't do it, you'll have to."

> Each emotion is like a country. Those who've
> suffered grief live in a different world/country than
> those who haven't.

Loft Apartment in the restaurant district, St Kilda, Melbourne

As far as we know no one has died here, but still at times and in low light it is hard to tell people from ghosts. Davey is often here. If I were to make a card of it, I would say:

This three-bedroom home built above a commercial space (dress shop, bookshop, antique shop, health food shop) is light and airy. The fittings are true to the era of construction, although the walls have been painted a number of times.

It has a large first bedroom, quite a big second, and an adequate third. A lounge room big enough for a couch and an armchair, opening onto the dining area. The table could be extended to seat fifteen or twenty, for those with large families who visit. The kitchen is a good size, with a light green linoleum floor.

We live in that loft apartment and run a small restaurant below. It's called Comfort and Joy. We are open until late because Mum can't sleep. She'll take a nap in the afternoon and that does her. Joy says she cooks better drunk, and that is probably the case. If she makes breakfast sober it is always bland and overcooked. I'm the one who does the breakfasts.

━✦━

We don't know what the purpose of the cards is. They must date back at least a couple of hundred years, but to who? To what? I don't have, won't have, the answers. I should have said that sooner. They are old, though. They've been drawing people in all this time, making them follow the deathplaces. Did Julie affect the cards from her sandy grave? Can they be changed like that?

Mum works her way through the cards. It's relentless and she is so very tired. She's been to a fifteenth-story tiny apartment in Brisbane (it was here that a young woman died of an overdose; prescription pills of some kind—she was found under the kitchen table, blood spurting up out of her mouth in a geyser). A motel in Wagga Wagga (sex worker murdered), a factory in Perth (industrial accident), a theater in Orange (fifteen dead in stage collapse). She's been to a dam in Waragamba and a dairy farm in Moe.

One card that never appeared is the one for Uncle Rufus, so I made it for her. I couldn't find the original artist, but all the others since copied that style (you can only tell the difference by a brush stroke here and there, by some of the colors chosen, and by the initials that will appear in the corner), and I tried to do the same. Using one of the cards, I made a clumsy drawing, and I wrote on the back all the stuff we know about Uncle Rufus and what he did and what happened next. It didn't magically turn into one of the deathplace cards and I felt as if I needed to thank God or whatever being was looking out for me. That was not a talent I wanted.

CARD 18/24
PUBLIC WARD, ST VINCENT'S HOSPITAL, SYDNEY

Built in 1857, this Catholic health provider serves the inner city of Sydney and is one of the busiest hospitals in Australia. This ward has twelve beds, each of them clean and neat, with the smell of antiseptic, the smell of nurses, the smell of warm food.

Those with support will die at home or in a hospice. Rufus Airlie had neither, although his brother Duncan sits by his bedside as the last moments approach. They did not have a close relationship, and Duncan looks at his watch, snaps at the staff, is anxious to get on with his business. Rufus was famous once, renowned, and still if you say his name in certain folk music circles they'll say, 'Whatever happened to him?'

Rufus confessed his sins to Duncan. He said, 'I killed that girl. She called herself Julietta but she was a Julie if I ever saw one. I didn't know she had a son. I killed her and buried her and her bones will never get home.'

'You leave them be,' he said. 'You don't even look. My name is our name and that's all our father gave us, Duncan.'

'She made me do it, I swear. It's like she was possessed, or I was.'

Duncan did find the body. He didn't report it. He just wanted to see if it was there. He didn't want to ruin his brother's name. He found the cards, resting under her elbow, and those he took because they gave him a good feeling.

He kept the cards safe and he visited so many of the places. He followed the cards. Until he jumped in front of a train and Gloria found them, but it was Jarrold who was the one taken by them.

Mum loved the card. She said, "I think those cards tried to get in my head early on but it never worked like it did with the men. Maybe that's why Davey got a hold on your father and not me. I didn't even see him. Didn't notice him. I feel a bit bad about that. We know you're there now, Davey! We see you!" Raising her voice and talking to him as if he was a son.

Anytime I thought I saw him he was younger than when he died, older than when his mum was murdered, about my age as if he was my twin, but that just confuses things.

Then Mum looked again at the cigarette cards, and there was a new one, and she packed her small bag and took off.

━╱╎╲━

We'd paid for Julie's remains to join her son Davey. You'd think (in a story where all the ends were tied up it would be) that this would be him at peace and that he wouldn't need any more from us. You'd think he'd had enough from us, with just me, Mum and Joy left of the whole family. I wonder if I summoned him, when I had that séance at school? But that doesn't seem right. He summoned us, I think, to find that café, and helped us stay there long enough so that he could wrap himself around Dad and seek revenge. He tried for Mum. Tried to possess her but it wasn't happening, and did those sacrifices mean we found out about Julie and the burial?

‐✦‐

I always make an extra plate of breakfast for whoever I can't see. I always place a glass of wine or a bottle of beer on the counter in the evening. Sometimes if the light is right I'll see them, in amongst the living. Slouched in the booths or slumped against the counter. Or leaning against the wall. I don't know any of them except Davey, who doesn't seem angry but will not leave. If I can figure out how to send him to Hell I will.

WE CALLED IT GRAFFITIVILLE

AARON DRIES

PART ONE
THE WAVE

"We'll only ever know the places
Those mountains and the faces
And each and every view
I love for the worlds I walked with you."

—Dom King Come, *Our Mile*

33

THE WAVE WORE a mask of faces, some screaming, others silent. Broken arms and legs and necks butterflied by windows and car doors. Tin roofs twisted into spears. Glass. Metal. Knots of wire. Dead babies and bricks rolled on bloody, pink sea foam. Sharks with their lower jaws ripped off landed on the road before being sucked into the vortex again. Motorbikes. Chairs. Trees fell behind us, launching coconut grenades at our backs. We ran as fast as we could. We screamed. The wave wore many faces, but it was ours it wanted most.

This can't be happening, I remember thinking. *Not to people like us.*

We're good.

A loud thought cut through the crashing, coach's curdled Greek voice saying, *You skips are all the same. Malakas. Oi, look at me, Dan. Look me in the eye. Being good don't mean shit in the end. Being good gets you out of nothin'.*

32

Questioner: Deep breaths, Daniel. Remember we want you to succeed.

Interviewee: Ha, okay. Dan's fine. And yeah, I'm ready. Ready as I'll ever be.

Questioner: Thanks for meeting with us. Opportunities like these don't come up all that often. There were many applications, as you can imagine. The overall quality of the candidates was high. Our successful applicant will be staring down the barrel of a twenty-seven-month posting, not including three months of intensive in-country training. This training mostly involves learning the language, getting your head around all the cultural norms, that kind of thing. To say many people, especially people your age, find this part of being a volunteer quite the haul would be an understatement. But that's still the easy bit. Once you're in-country, isolation can catch you off guard. So, make friends where you can. Lean on the other volunteers if there are any stationed near you. On the flipside, a lack of privacy can be rough. You might go from having your own room here to sharing with a dozen people in poor living quarters there. You might have to set aside what you believe in, the ideals you subscribe to that you wouldn't otherwise tolerate when it comes to, say, gender, or the status of minorities. It's important you're made aware of all this in advance. We need the right people for this posting, Dan. The world's a wild place. And often in ways our volunteers never see coming.

Interviewee: I'm ready. I really am.

Questioner: That's good to hear. Look. Your application was strong. We can see how passionate you are. Your local community efforts are top-notch, too. And quite the sportsman. I've played a bit of tennis in my day as well. A man after my own heart. I digress.

Questioner Two: He does that.

Interviewee: I've learned a lot on the courts. You break your back training and then there comes a point when you just know you're ready to take it to the next level. When you know, you know. Well, I'm ready to take this, all of this, to the next level.

Questioner: When you know, you know.

Interviewee: Yeah.

Questioner: I like that, Dan.

Questioner Two: What we're asking you is this: Why do you want to join the Corps? Feel free to be frank with us.
Interviewee: Because I give a shit.

31

Kiki and I visited To Sua Ocean Trench the afternoon before the wave, a thirty-metre swimming hole in a lava field near Lotofaga Village on the southern island of Upolo. There were, in fact, two pools, each linked by a canal the ocean submerged when the tide was high. Members of our scrawny and sunburned deployment said only the brave dipped below the surface and allowed themselves to be sucked through the narrow chute, hopeful they'll pop out the other side—a rite of passage for tourists, according to the dog-eared travel guides in our Apia office. Locals said only the stupid would try. The tide was high when we arrived, as if by design. A good thing for guys who always have something to prove. Guys like me.

I glanced at Kiki, daring her to tell me to stop. We treaded water, an icy torrent between us. Mixed-language calls from other visitors echoed off the fern-laced walls of the hole in the earth in the middle of nowhere in a speck in the Pacific. Screaming birds. Insect drone, constant and summery. These sounds defined me now, here in-country, and so far from whatever passed for home in Australia.

My girlfriend half-smiled back at me. I caught a glimpse of the silver tooth set into her lower jaw. It was the first thing I noticed about her at initiation. I called it her diamond at the bottom of the lake. The shape of Kiki's face, everything about her, was a solicitation without an obligation to let you in. I adored how she owed me nothing. Kiki glanced away, flipping water from her brow, a simple gesture that felt like a goodbye.

I hungered to tell Kiki I loved her, but kept my mouth shut. Saying 'love' aloud changed its meaning. Better to bottle it up instead, and in private, cup that bottle with my palms and enjoy the heat it emitted. Throwing the word around (as I'd done for too long) lamed an otherwise powerful thing. *Love you—oh, and don't forget to lock the back door. Love you, sleep tight, don't let the bed bugs bite. Love you.* Numb. *Love.* Blunt. *Love.* Dead. I dipped below the surface, pinching my nose, eyes squeezed tight. And cupped the bottle, felt its gentle warmth. Mourned the inert loves I'd thrown about when things were good between us, back when Kiki and I treated each other better.

You can do this, Dan. Show her how brave you are.

(Or foolish. Coach's voice again. *Malaka.)*

The tide sucked me under. I kept my left hand on my forehead in case I bumped the rocky ceiling. It wasn't far, ten yards at most, but that airless canal might have been the length of two back-to-back football fields in the dark. The slimy knots of the rope strung between the trenches scraped my shoulder as I passed through. Later, I'd use that rope to pull myself back to the main trench, the only safe exit to the jungle above—assuming I made it. Brightness bloomed in the water. I popped out the other side, gasping for oxygen, snot dribbling from my nose. Alive and thankful.

You're a fucking skip idiot, mate.

The owner of that voice often stumbled over his insults, speaking like he rolled knuckles from cheek to cheek. I could still see his face. The thick lips. Olive skin. Brow pebbled with sweat. It didn't matter what he did with his hair; by training's end, the cowlick always won out. *Fuch-hing-eed-iot.* That had been Coach's way of putting me in my place, pressing me into something he needed with meaty Greek fingers. His prints on my life would never go away. I guess you could call that affection.

If you're so desperate to off yourself, do it for you and you alone. Not to impress a girl who doesn't want you no more. That's how broken you both are. Oi, look at me, Dan. Look me in the eye. Dumb skip bastard.

Applause filled the cave. I turned in the water and saw a local man on the pebbled shore, the saltwater stinging my eyes and making the sheen of his brown skin glow in the light filtering through the rock cleft above.

"Well done, uso," he said.

Uso: The Samoan word for brother.

"Thanks," I said. "Should be someone else coming through any—"

Kiki's pale skin in the water, fish belly white. A star of red hair. She broke the surface like she'd lived this life before, totally calm, this elegant thing, and maybe doing so was a way of keeping me at a disadvantage. My chest loosened.

"We did it," I said, fist-pumping the air.

"Sure did," Kiki said in a clipped tone, brightening when she saw the Samoan man watching us. She lifted a hand to him and paddled past me. Her heat in the water, there and gone. I joined them on a seat of shells and dead starfish.

The cave walls were ornamented with purple crabs that skittered into a frenzy whenever we spoke. Their chatter complemented the *swoosh* of water, our breaths between greetings. I studied the tribal signals on the man's skin, his Pe'a. Samoan tatau was tied to myth that reached far beyond the missionaries who changed the way of life here in the 1800s. Complex Polynesian legacy with its worshipping of nature was, with time, converted to Christianity. As a foreigner who came to this country to make a difference, this was a history I'd never been comfortable with. It made me question why I was here in the first place. They sent me to Samoa to help. But help is a bit like cannibalism.

Help them all the way down to the bone.

We sat with the stranger for ten minutes, Kiki and I talking about the community projects we'd collaborated on, listing the schools we worked at, explaining how I taught kids to play tennis as a way of keeping them engaged in class. His expression dropped when we told him of our plans for the following morning.

"Cool, cool, just be careful," he said. "Yeah?"

Kiki and I planned to scale a long-dead volcano by the coast, one overgrown with jungle, at the foot of which a tourist nook had been erected. We were going to head to our basic accommodation there after climbing out of the trench that afternoon.

Mount Foliga.

"Most mountains go like this," he said, tilting his arm at a 45-degree angle. "That's Mount Vaea back in Apia. This one, though, uso. It's like this." He raised his arm to a full 90 degrees. "That's why they call it 'Foliga'. Flat as a face looking back at you, a face looking over the ocean. Valea, eh?"

Valea: Crazy.

"We'll be right," I said. "We're fit. And Kiki and I like the risk. Don't we, babe?"

"I guess we do."

"Cool, cool," he said. "There are rainwater pools in the craters up there. Take a swim, just don't stay long."

"We read online that there's a special type of fish in those pools," Kiki said. "Like, these big goldfish. And the water's so clear you can see them right next to you as if they're swimming in the air. Supposed to be awesome."

The Samoan man cracked the bones in his hands. He wore a little crucifix on a chain about his neck. "Sure," he said. "See the fishes, and then get back down the cliff. Don't go over the other side of the mountain, in the bowl of the crater." He put the crucifix to his lips. "We was always told it's not safe up there. The ground is—what's the word?—it's not, like, steady. The earth is loose."

"We'll be careful," I said, the warning only motivating me more. I don't know why I was letting the dude-bro valor take hold of me when I resented it so much in other men. "We're brave."

"Yeah, all you palangis are brave," he said, nudging me in the ribs. "And you must've been brave to come through to this cave."

"Or really, really dumb," Kiki said, smiling. "Palangi pride."

We shared a laugh.

"Maybe," the Samoan man said, wiping his brow. His hands were huge. "My uncle used to tell me how back in the old times, warriors would swim between these two caves when the tide was high as a test of their courage. A lot of people drowned, or fell when climbing out of the main trench. The warriors who made it said they were ready to face God, that they'd proven themselves worthy to stand in His shadow."

Hearing this didn't surprise me. In the months I'd been in-country, I'd heard similar tales, all origin stories, the myths behind every mountain and rock pool. There were superstitions in every house. Old rituals, village orators appointed to communicate sacred words and spiritual decree. This was all the remaining fabric of a world white people with their white religion hadn't ripped to shreds and braided into something familiar, which now only just survived and existed in tandem with imported knock-off clothes from Bali and warring mobile phone companies and a McDonald's restaurant in Apia where they often ran out of stock and only sold chicken nuggets. This was Samoa to a T. And I loved it.

Kiki and I lived in a secure compound in Mo'tua'tua, walking distance from the Robert Louis Stevenson memorial, with four other volunteers and a cat that answered to Brucey. The Australian Corps, satisfied with giving us a stipend to cover food and not much else, hired a housecleaner named Atamai to ensure we didn't trash the place. She scolded us for putting coconut cream in our curries, taught us how to cook with breadfruit from the trees outside, and once slapped a broom out of my hands while I swept the kitchen floor after dinner.

"You can't do that," she'd said, eyes wide and shimmering.

"Jesus Christ, why not?"

"Sweeping after dark brings ghosts. They like the sound. Especially ghosts that want revenge on you. And Dan, don't blaspheme. Not in this house. It's not yours. It's our home."

Laughing this off came easy at the time. Later that night, however, in my bed beneath the mosquito net with Kiki snoring into her pillow, two yellow eyes floated in the darkness outside our (their) window. My skin broke into goosebumps. Waking Kiki wasn't an option. *She'll think you're a pussy,* I could almost hear Coach whispering, his lips pressed against the mosquito net, wet with spit. Instead, I watched those eyes until they receded into the night. Every minute passed in my bones, in every heartbeat, with morning far away. The crunch of brush chickens walking over the deadfall sounded like men with machetes. Bark grinding against bark were giggles at my expense. Every coconut dropped from the trees: a cough in the throat of someone growing impatient with waiting, ready to make their move. Samoan night is either sweet or brutal, with little in between. I swore I'd never sweep after dark again.

$$\text{--}/\text{I}\text{\textbackslash--}$$

"And are you?" Kiki said to the man beside us in the cave, her voice almost drowned out by the thrumming water. Mildew shimmered in the dusky light.

"What?" said the man. "Am I ready to face God? Is that what you're asking?"

"Yeah, bro," she said, sounding a bit like me. An inwards cringe.

The man laughed, and that laugh released tension I hadn't noticed coiled inside me. "Born ready," he said, sticking out his tongue and lifting his right hand to give us a Hang-Ten, thumb and little finger raised. It aged him somehow.

"Want to come with us tomorrow?" Kiki said.

That stung. She knew I'd planned for the climb to be just us. Our end—

(and that's what this is, silly boy, you skip)
—would have been neater if one of us had cheated, or if there had been words that couldn't be taken back. Something *finite*. Kiki rotted in silence that wasn't silence. I hated how my presence hurt her. It only made me want to offer more comfort. Realizing you've become someone else's cancer is a terrible thing, that you need to be cut from their lives for fear of them sickening beyond the hope of healing.

It wasn't as if I'd dragged her—kicking and screaming—out of Apia. Sure, we'd planned the weekend away months ago, but at any point she could have said, *Go on your own, Dan. I don't want to be there with you.*

We're so done.

No, we loaded up the old car instead, only for us to have to change the tire somewhere between the compound and our destination. I drew a six-inch nail out of the rubber tread by the side of the road. You didn't travel far from Apia without first mastering the art of tire changing—and quick smart, too, before the wild dogs with the sagging teats and a static cloud of fleas hovering about them came sniffing. We soldiered on, the songs we used to sing staining the air as we drove, me hitting skip on *Our Mile* by Dom King Come. The lyrics had soured. We used to dance to that beat. Now our outwards energy slammed inwards instead, bruising us from within.

I should've pulled the pin and let her let me go.

But I can't.

Chicken shit is what I am. Coach was right. He always was.

"Hell no, I'm not coming with you," the Samoan man said, standing, brushing shards of broken starfish off his board shorts. "My cousins would kill me. I'd wake up sipping kava in heaven. No fun there, uso. No fun."

We watched him dive into the pool and climb close to the wall, using the rope to spider-swim his way back to the trench. The clap of his skin against the water circled the walls in his absence, crabs in riot, the sound like a *hell-no, hell-no, hell-no*, scaling higher, fading, fading, and hungry for light.

30

We sprawled on the wooden floor of the faleo'o hut at the foot of the ocean, having turned in before midnight.

Pound. And. Sigh.

I hadn't noticed the waves because we'd had a good time at the bar across the road, accustomed to the sound as I had been my heartbeat. Or at least *I* thought we'd had a good time. Now, the pound and the sigh of the waves was everywhere, closer than it should have been, hardly a sigh at all but a crashing instead. An angry ocean.

Hot air felt too tight on my skin as I waited in the dark for Kiki to stop pretending I wasn't there.

Clicking eyelids. A whistle in my nose. How the leaf-thatched roof rustled in the wind. And the Pacific, always the Pacific, pounding and sighing, and I realized then that whatever fun we'd had that night had been a distraction. I never used to notice these things. Not when I was around her.

"Kiki?" I said.

Pound. And. Sigh.

"Yeah?" Her reply was a question and not a question.

Pound. And. Sigh.

My throat was dry. "I can hear you thinking."

The hut smelled of the Taula Strong beer we'd consumed during karaoke with the locals. If I drew aside our mosquito net and squinted into the dark—our dark—I'd see the dinky bar set against Mount Foliga with its flat face that watched over the ocean, not that it would alert us to danger. Foliga, we would soon learn, was passive, apathetic, as though *still* recovering from the toll of blowing her top a hundred-and-fifty years prior. There on that dance floor, Kiki and I offered awkward smiles to the backpackers we'd met who said we were so cute together. They didn't see us now, but as we used to be.

A few locals kept the party going, men in lavalava skirts and Quicksilver T-shirts who swayed with microphones that cut out without warning, belting Reggae Christmas songs even though it was September, disco lights throwing their shadows around the walls. In Samoa, carols chimed from homes and grocery markets from August onwards. That was just the way things were here.

"Want to climb in with me?" I said, shuffling my sleeping bag. "It's warmerrrrrrr?"

"It's, like, a billion degrees, Dan."

Her back to me. I wanted her touch. Was I horny? Yes. But it wasn't about that. I couldn't let it be about that. It was as if my veins were leaping out of my flesh to net her, catch her, not to consume her but to be wrestled into submission by her. Only if she said yes.

"Do you have any painkillers?" Kiki said. "I don't want to wake up with a hangover. The hike will be hard enough as it is."

So she was worried about tomorrow, too. Good. That's how starved I was for something in common. "In the pocket of my backpack by your head. Can you feel it?"

Impatient crunching in the dark, and then brightness. I rolled onto my back. There were gecko silhouettes at the bottom of the paper shade of the overhead light, gummy feet like Garfield suction cups in car windows back in Australia. Kiki and I referred to geckos as 'land dolphins' on account of the sounds they made. We had names for everything. Secret maps and words and insignificant things we stumbled across, the unimportant things we infused with importance, our way of making them our own. Stealing things. Colonizing things to capture in TikToks and Instagram posts for likes and shares. If you didn't validate it somehow, it didn't exist.

Electricity buzzed in the hut. The crinkle of foil. An unscrewed bottle. Kiki's throat clenching as she swallowed again and again.

"Better?" I said.

"I'm tired, Dan," she said—not unkindly though.

Click. And darkness once more.

These moments are so clear to me now. Slivers of life.

We didn't speak for the rest of the night. I checked my phone, which had been charging within reach. The huts may be rudimentary, but they were designed for palangi, foreigners like us, after all. Just because we weren't tourists didn't mean we were any less obnoxious than other off landers. It was after twelve and I had a single bar of reception—pretty good considering how remote we were on that part of the island.

Music thrummed on, a cha-cha beat that followed me out of the hut and along the beach. The moon broke into a billion pieces on the water. A cat near the unpaved road meowed my way before being chased off by a dog. I was drawn to a bonfire where three

Samoan guys and a handsome fa'afafine sat drinking beers and laughing, the men noodling with guitars.

"Talofa lava," I said. It felt nice (and if not nice, then at least *different* enough to feel in the neighborhood of nice) to not be feared upon first viewing. Back in Australia, were I to approach a group on a beach in such a manner (let alone at night), I'd find myself in a citizen's arrest, uploaded to YouTube within minutes, the footage sold to a major outlet before anyone asked me my name. Here in Samoa, foreignness was a kind of celebrity I struggled to reconcile. Walking into town from Mo'tua'tua, kids would rush out of their houses at the encouragement of their parents to touch my arms, asking me to play sports with them, those little hands dragging me back to the family home where I'd then be invited to a wedding the following weekend. I never accepted, though other volunteers had. It didn't seem right.

"Malo, uso," said the youngest of the men. They invited me to join them and handed me a beer I necked straight from the bottle. Warm. Tasted like sweat sucked from knots of hair. I answered their questions and laughed at their jokes and sang when they sang. They loved that I was in the Corps and thanked me for the work I'd done on Savai'i, how I'd engaged the kids with tennis. They all had family in that area, and asked me to show them the Ash Barty slice, me pantomiming how to hold a tennis racquet and swishing by firelight. They wanted to know if I had a girlfriend, and if I didn't if I was in the market for a Samoan wife. I was drawn into a hug when I told them about Kiki, and how I thought we were over. These strangers on the beach were the first and only people I had said that aloud to. Most Samoan men and women, especially after a few drinks, were kind beyond compare. They lived large, unashamed to embrace your hurt away. The word 'love' didn't seem to devalue when said aloud by them. Sometimes, I wondered what it was in this country that needed aid, that required the bleeding hearts of people like us.

We drank for an hour. They told me I was crazy for planning to hike up the mountain.

"Go up," the fa'afafine said, their face cupped from both sides by moonlight and flame glow. "And then come straight back down. Do that, and you'll be okay."

My brain said: *Thank you. I'm not going to remember that.*

Deliberately.

Hands were shaken, invites to join them the following night for drinks extended but passed on. Tomorrow was Sunday, and Kiki and I had to be back in Apia for work on Monday. Only there would be no following night. Not for these nice people.

The karaoke bar was closed by the time I headed for the hut. Waves pounded and sighed at my left. The air was thick, like breathing through damp cheesecloth. An eight-inch-long centipede crossed my path, leaving a series of frowns and smiles in the sand. My skin crawled with it. There was nothing in Samoa I hated more than the giant centipede—even worse than the dogs I had to ward off with sticks or rocks—an aggressive critter that would fight anything it could find. They had a nasty habit of climbing into beds and biting people while they slept. Their venom wasn't deadly, though the pain severe enough to often result in a visit to Tupua Tamasese Meaole Hospital. I'd avoided bites, but other volunteers hadn't been so fortunate. One scaled Kiki's inner thigh while we were posing for photographs at the house, sinking its incisors into the flesh beneath her swimming bottoms. I comforted Kiki for hours, wrapping ice cubes in tea towels and daubing her leg, bringing her cups of tea, and after two in the morning, something stronger. There was, of course, no sweeping.

No.

None of that.

I left the centipede, secure in the fact that our hut was erected on poles dug deep into the sand. My eyes turned to the horizon and the ring of coral half a mile from shore. Waves broke on the rocky fringe, the strip of white resembling bleached liner on an eye that never blinked, which only ever stared. That eye versus Mount Foliga. The two challenging each other, maybe. *Come at me, bro.* No clouds that night. Silver bioluminescence from the algae bloom of plankton shone in the waves as they curled and crashed.

It was my turn to sigh. I loved this country, even if I didn't understand it. Samoa. Pronounced Sa-Moa. The name translated to sacred (*sa*) and moa (*chicken*). Headscratcher, but sure. Samoa didn't understand me either. I feared the day when I would have to leave and return to Adelaide with my tail between my legs. There was a terrible ache in my core, too, the sick knowledge that those remaining months would be spent alone. I pissed into the wind, and cock in hand, thought about how Kiki had come away with me to make it clear she didn't need me anymore. Assuming she ever did.

Ocean to my left. Mountain on my right.

Kiki and I with our little dramas in between.

29

Questioner: Is giving a damn enough, though? A lot of young people care about others. But those young people—people of any age, really—aren't whittling their lives down into a suitcase, saying goodbye to all their loved ones, and gallivanting to developing countries. No. If anything, they're battening down the hatches. We don't want people to bring their emotional baggage into these vulnerable communities. It's too risky for everyone involved.

Questioner Two: Our ideal candidate is someone who can disconnect themselves from who they used to be. It's a survival technique, you could say.

Interviewee: I can disconnect.

Questioner: And your family, Dan? How would they react to you being sent to some foreign country on the other side of the world? You can be honest with us.

Interviewee: I'm not leaving anyone behind.

28

Kiki and I set up the mountain at dawn. We'd been tempted to snooze our alarms. She'd smelled the booze glazing my body, and to prove a point, teased me until I schlepped out of the hut to join her on the sand. Sprite, she was. No observable hangover at all. One of *those* people.

"This was your idea and we're not backing out because you drank yourself stupid last night," she said, sliding into her hiking boots—a little slower than she did other mornings. *Gotcha.* Maybe not as sober as she wanted me to think.

Not that I called her out.

"I feel fine," I lied, gripping a towel. "Give me five to—"

A wave of the hand. That's all I had in me.

I threw up in the public toilets across the street next to the bar, and had a quick shower. Hot water was a luxury I hadn't experienced in fourteen months. The cold shock did wonders that morning. I shoveled down a quick breakfast—a bread roll, a few Tylenols, and a bottle of Coke instead of coffee. Desperate times called for desperate measures. The day had dawned flawless and striking, a kind of summons for everything to turn wicked. No warning needed. But that's tragedy for you.

That's disaster.

Kiki led the way. My girlfriend didn't suffer fools lightly. Maybe she had a right to be angry. She hadn't poured the drinks down my throat. I didn't have to expect sympathy to want it.

"Hard part's over," I joked, following her up the mountain a shaky step at a time. "Right?"

"Nope."

Kiki was incapable of lying. Not even when I wanted her to.

We're here in Samoa because it's such a good cause, many of the volunteers said in those early weeks—bumper-sticker bullshit that stopped us from quitting when being so far from home played on us more than we thought it would, when being unable to navigate the culture or language tipped from adventure to alienation.

It's all so worthwhile. What we're doing is meaningful. We're making a difference.

Kiki called me out on this.

She turned to me a few days into our deployment, sipping a beer on a Sunday afternoon (an offence that would have seen us booted back to our respective homes had we been caught) and said, "I can't handle how fake so many of you guys are."

"Why are you here then?" I asked, accepting her beer when she offered it. Tonguing the rim as she'd done, her saliva in my mouth. She giggled at my don't-rock-the-boat naïveté. Kiki intimidated me from the start, and I liked how small she made me feel. It reminded me of Coach, I guess.

"For the same reason you are. Because back home we're nothing. We're potatoes under a sink going all soft and sprouting roots. Here in Samoa, we kind of matter. Come on, dude, it's not like we're teaching kids how to speak English *just* for them. We're doing it because it makes us feel worthy." Her knowing smile stretched too wide, showing off her silver tooth, the diamond at the bottom of the ocean, and I sensed hurt in her. I wanted to probe further but didn't, not then. That would come later. I never got the answers I sought, the mystery at her middle, but she sensed my hunger to understand her through touch, in the ways I kissed her, the places I kissed her. "I don't know about you, Dan, but I could do with a little self-worth." She sipped the beer she'd snatched back. Slop in the bottle.

No lies. No sympathy. Just muscle and move on.

The mountain above was two things at once: steep but not as high as expected. Were we to knuckle down, we might reach the top quite quickly.

Kiki's strides were strong, hard to match. The path zig-zagged up the incline, marked by branches that had been sawed back with machetes, slimy rocks that shifted under our weight. Hand-sized butterflies zipped between us. And the air was thick with the almost fecal richness of overripe papaya. It didn't matter the time of the year or what you were doing; you sweated through the daylight hours, and that morning proved no different. A mix of sunscreen and bug dope dripped into my eyes. *Sting.* I pushed on, quiet.

Scat rained over us a few minutes later.

We shielded our faces and glanced to the sky. Hundreds of birds flew in circles. Their screams came first, followed by rumbling I felt in my tooth fillings. Human screams came last.

27

Questioner: Are you saying there's nobody who'd be waiting for you to get back?

Interviewee: Friends, sure. But they get it. They want to get out of Adelaide, too. I don't see much of my parents anymore. We, uh, don't have the best relationship. That makes leaving easier, honestly.

Questioner: Sorry to hear that, Dan. Any siblings?

Interviewee: No.

26

I remember my parents telling me we were expecting a baby girl, and the shock that came later when they delivered a boy instead.

Mum could have delivered a bullfrog and they would have greeted him with love. The miscalculation by her physician required our grandmother to throw away all the pink booties she'd knitted with her arthritic fingers and start buying blue yarn in bulk. Mum and Dad named the baby Cory. I loved my brother before he was born, even when we thought he was going to be a girl. And I loved him even more when I saw him.

To me, and I assume others, memories aren't consecutive. It's all a mosaic. Something whole shattered into pieces. There's no meaning in the mess. This is just how the mind works. The sharpest edges remain nearest.

I can still see Cory coming up to our parents at a barbeque in our backyard, and how he told them he needed to pee, and my father saying, You're the big brother, Dan, now take him to the toilet and show him how it's done.

And then there's Cory letting go of Mum's hand at K-Mart, not staying put like she asked him to, how he roamed wild from the second her head was tilted away, how we lost him in the store. The sounds of his cries bouncing off mannequins and action figures. I followed these echoes and found Cory under a coat rack, surrounded by strangers trying to coax him out. I swiped at these women and men with my fists and let Cory spill into my arms. His cheek pressed against mine. He couldn't have been older than two and a half at the time. Cory looked at me and I could hear the voice I imagined he'd one day have, and that voice told me how he thought he'd be lost in K-Mart forever. That he would grow old in there.

There is also the memory of Cory propped up in his booster seat in the backseat of our family car. The whip of windscreen wipers slashing left to right. Paradise by the Dashboard Light *on the radio. Whenever it played, which wasn't often—sometimes at a party my parents threw in the shed or when they took us to the golf club with their friends (where we kids weren't allowed to cross a certain line in the carpet, adults only from that point on)— Cory and I knew we didn't exist. The song was long and dramatic and made me nervous. It signaled how alone we could be. We were kids and needed attention for fear of not existing, because at that age, who were we if we were not being endorsed in some way? It's possible this trait followed me into my teens and beyond. I knew every word to that song, even if I didn't like singing it. Maybe I was too afraid not to know the words.*

Dad was driving that night. Mum smelled of white wine. They both did. It was summer and I was nine years old. The memory is sharp.

25

The wave came fast.

I screamed for us to run, adrenalin pounding—not that Kiki would have heard me. The thundering sound behind us felt solid enough to shake clouds from the sky. We scrambled up the incline.

This isn't happening, I told myself. *This isn't real.*

(you're not half as good as you think you are, you skip)

The heels of Kiki's shoes were matted with wet earth, stained green from the grass. Real colors. I snatched at vines to propel myself forward. Real bark clenched in my palms. Gravity pushed, pushed. Spiders in Kiki's hair. She'd tied it back before leaving, using the remains of a faded Australian Corps shirt, the logo peeking through her bangs. The shirt tumbled free. I trod it into the mud. The mud, too, was real.

Our faleo'o huts were the first to go, followed by shanties where villagers lived, some hosting tourists. Now all dead or dying. The bar where we'd danced the night before was shredded, electricity sparking as powerlines went down. The wave chewed through everything below, spinning people in its tide. It didn't matter who you were. All jelly now.

Kiki's backpack swung from side to side, elbows jabbing the air. I pushed her on, picked her up when she fell. Kiki was all bones and pulse. Her hand on my arm dug deep. If I could have crawled inside her, I would have. She had saved me many times over. It was Kiki who helped me the morning I woke in the taxi stand after drinking too much watching the World Cup, my wallet and sandals thieved in the night. I deserved it when she called me a bloody idiot in the car. I *had* been a bloody idiot. There was safety in her honesty.

Men, women, and children climbed the hill behind us.

They never stood a chance.

Water and metal and meat and wood crashed against the mountain wall, surging high. I heard its suck. The jungle shrieked. Snakes slipped from branches. We were close to the top of the crater where birds rode the wind. Rocks dislodged beneath our boots. Three wild boars ran in front of us, slipped and tumbled by our heads, a tusk whizzing past my eye. The animals rolled, squealing, into the Pacific at our heels.

An old woman was thrown from the torrent and landed beside me. Her head cracked open. Memories of children, weddings, the funerals of those she'd survived, recipes, knitting patterns, weavings, and a billion kisses reduced to brain sludge on my thighs.

I saw the old woman. I did not see the old woman.

24

I saw Cory. He looked like one of the drawings you saw on Christmas cards. That's how cute he was. And tall for a five-year-old, too. Fidgety. He pushed against the seatbelt crossing his chest, thrashing as if dancing to the song, even though he wasn't. Mum and Dad were still singing. I hated it when they sang like that, as if they were shouting or angry. It embarrassed me even though we were the only ones in the car. Or maybe I was just tired. Not that I'd admit it. Kid rule number one.

We wove along the windy bush road between wherever we were and home.

A drink bottle rattled in the door holster.

The ongoing clunk-clunk as Cory pushed against his seatbelt.

Rain pummeled the roof. Mum and Dad called the car Betty White because "The thing just keeps on trucking!" Whatever that meant.

It was dark. I remember seeing the crown of Dad's bald head looming above the headrest in front of me, and how his scalp looked like a rising moon.

My brother kept thrashing against the seat belt.

Clunk. Clunk-clunk. Clunk.

Cory cried. My parents sang, breathless and sweaty and drunk and making the car smell of alcohol and me breathing in the stink. Their love for the song hinted at a history I wasn't a part of, good times from the photos of them when they were younger, skinnier versions of themselves, trapped under wax paper. I was jealous they had what I wanted: age. And I resented them for having outgrown everything my brother and I knew to be real.

Mum and Dad didn't notice me doing what I knew I shouldn't be doing. But we didn't exist. There was only the song to them and what I imagined were the memories of who they used to be: people who didn't have children. The road ribboned out in front of us, headlight glow like eyes staring back through the windscreen.

23

Kiki heaved me upwards. Her mouth moved in the shape of MOVE-IT-DAN. Spittle on my face. The vibrations of her voice passed into me through her grip.

I spun away from the dead woman on the mountain.

We were almost at the dormant volcano's lip, further than we knew we should have gone, where the ground didn't hold, the birds close enough to touch. Earth rattled, proving the Samoan man's point from the day before in the cave where bravery was measured in held breaths. Boulders dislodged. Dirt mixed with sky mist. It didn't seem possible that the wave could reach such heights. My suspicion was correct.

The sound of receding water was almost industrial, a reminder of the coal mining fields back home where steam erupted from pipes. Liquid to fire. Things caught between cogs. The tide dropped, revealing bicycles in the trees. Beer bottles wrapped in seaweed. Television sets. Fish slipped out of bushes. An upturned car with its wheels pried off. Corpses sprawled here, there, all stripped of their clothes. A mile of death and broken glass below us.

Where there's one wave there can be another, I thought, locking eyes with Kiki. She knew it, too. The only way out was up. For now, at least.

Kiki and I forced ourselves through a line of trees and emerged on the crater's narrow rim where the air was colder. Birds twirled and divebombed. We dropped to our knees, crying and screaming. I hugged Kiki. She hugged me back, arms around arms, our salt mixing with sea spray and shit and mud and sap. I tried to speak but couldn't find the words, and when Kiki tried to answer I couldn't hear her.

Tinnitus.

Mist cleared. An unreal blue sky. Clouds parted to reveal an enormous bowl of foliage ahead, the crater's far side cusped in shadow by the still-rising sun. Help would come from that part of the island. Helicopters first, private charters accustomed to showing off beaches to tourists. Trucks, too—only they would take a while. From the public chicken busses to personal cars and emergency units, Samoan vehicles were write-offs from other countries. None of them did well with the terrain and were prone to breaking down—as Kiki and I knew too well. Not to mention the roads themselves, all limited to forty kilometers an hour, homing nasty nails and bales of wire that dropped off pickup flatbeds.

Every turn in those roads invited collision.

A month prior, one of the volunteers had been driving down a hill into a rural area too fast, and struck a sow in the middle of the street. It was later revealed that the pig had been part of a wedding dowry. This explained why the men in the village chased the volunteer out of town with machetes. Her car struggled up the hill, blades bouncing off her windows. She got there. Just. The volunteer sought refuge at the Australian embassy in Apia, where reimbursement of the dowry became a matter of diplomatic urgency. The volunteer was sent home without an opportunity to defend herself.

The ringing in my ears began to subside.

22

I stretched my arm across the no-mans-land that was the middle seat. Like quicksand in the adventure books I read, the more you moved the more the seatbelt tightened around your chest. That was what was happening to my brother. Drowning. I hated seeing Cory struggle. Those K-Mart cries. My fingers touched the orange button that would release his belt.

21

Kiki's voice broke through. "What do we do?" I caught a whiff of the mint gum she'd been chewing. It smelled artificial. "W-w-will someone send help, Dan?"

Earth shifted beneath our feet.

20

I depressed the button on Cory's belt. At the same time, a kangaroo bounced out in front of the car. I caught its glare, though my parents did not. Twin hole eyes in the night. The animal leapt up and backwards, launching into our windscreen hindquarters first. Glass shattered, threading my parents with scars they carry to this day. Dad hit the brakes. Betty White drifted across the wet road. Slammed into a tree. Inertia sent Cory flying out of the booster seat and through the windshield, pinwheeling like a doll tossed from a crib. He made no sound.

19

The lip of the crater crumbled. We rode the landslide into the bowl of the volcano, rolling as the soil rolled, thrown against trees as they toppled, coat-hangered by branches. The rollercoaster-dive stomach rush forced vomit out my nose. Kiki was ripped from my hands. Dust swallowed me up. Sod in my eyes, in my mouth. Stinking vegetation, spoiled fruit. No wind in the dust, no birds. Just the *BOOM* of rock against rock until I heard nothing at all.

18

Mum and Dad didn't move as I screamed and slapped at them within the crumpled car. They only moaned. Moaning was good. Moaning meant they were alive. The radio droned on, but the voices were fuzzy. Whispery leftovers of their song.

I unbuckled my belt. The door on my side opened easier than I expected it to.

My hand flat against the tarmac.

Cows cried, desperate for milking, on a hill. They looked like shadow puppets against the moon. Blue crayon drawing clouds.

The ground was hard. Toothy rocks bit into my palms as I crawled to where the bitumen ended and the grass began, like the line where the carpet ended at the golf club. Consequences beyond. Things that were for grown-ups only.

Tears peeled down my face as I scuttled forward. Cory was face-down on the ground beside the kangaroo. The animal's legs were bent backwards. It screeched into the wet night. My brother silent, still. Everything was lit in the harsh glow of the one headlight that hadn't busted open. My shadow fell long across a field.

I reached my brother and grabbed him by the shoulder. His name slipped out of me as I turned him over. His baby skin was clammy, frog-like. He was heavier than he'd ever felt when we wrestled over toys and fought for pretend territory in the backyard. A smell wafted off him, the smell of your hands after holding coins for too long. The road had worn Cory's face down to a nub. Glass shards for eyes. No mouth where there should be a mouth, the hole of his throat filling with rain. No gurgle. Just a red bubble in the knot.

Pop.

PART TWO
THE TOWN

"Have you been here before?
Razor pages from a forgotten lore
Let me tell it to you true
I now fear the worlds I walked with you."

—Dom King Come, *Our Mile*

17

A tickle on my tongue. Bolted awake. Gagged.

I flipped onto my stomach, every muscle straining, and spat what I thought were leaves onto the mud I was sinking into. A saliva-dewy praying mantis glared back at me, twitching its head before taking to the air. That something so small had survived something so enormous made zero sense to me. It flew away. Meanwhile, I writhed in earth like a split worm trying to knot itself back together again.

Breathe.

Drew oxygen into my system. Not easy. Wrong shaped air. I coughed. Everything sizzled bright. Bleach sky. Dirt all shiny and wet. The blood on my arms was red as jam oozing from a sandwich your mother makes you on the days she decides you're worth acknowledging, back before you run away from home for the first time.

Am I deaf? Oh, Jesus, no. Not that. Anything but that.

"—aaaaaaannnnnnnnnnnn!"

No, not deaf then.

Again. *"Daaaaaaaaaaaaaaaaaaaannnn!"*

Pain flared as I yanked my arms from the mud. Slipping. Sliding sideways. A sucking sound. I pinched my eyes shut, and in the dark, saw the ocean smashing the base of Mount Foliga again—how it climbed after us. I tried to tame the memory with my jaws, by crunching all the sand between my teeth. Granules popping. I hocked crunchy phlegm onto my hand. Blood in the mix. The wave receded for now.

"Help," I said aloud. It was like I could see the word popping out of my mouth and hovering in the air before being carried off by the wind. Coughed again.

Wood had speared my side in the fall, the shirt torn in patches. I looked at my feet and flashed back to that morning at the taxi stand with my grubby toes speaking of the prior night's stupid decisions, and how Kiki came to my rescue. Thankfully, my hiking boots were still strapped to my ankles this time. I hadn't been fleeced. Then again, I hadn't been so stupid. I—we—didn't deserve this. This hadn't come about because of a lapse in judgement. Nobody deserved what happened. This I told myself. Yet still felt punished.

No helicopters yet.

How long have I been out? Thirty seconds? Thirty minutes?

"DAN!"

Answer her, Coach said in his clunky accent.

I filled my lungs with air again (a sickly jab of agony in my side) and shouted Kiki's name. The effort emptied me out. I steadied myself, worried a faint was coming on.

"KIKI! Where are you?"

My gaze settled on her as though guided there: Kiki further down the incline, reedy in her rags. It took strength to wave my arms, but I did it. *Good. Don't give up. Coach would want you to fight*—even though I desired to make myself invisible, curl up into a ball, become a tiny thing. The world was too dangerous to let anyone know you existed. Better to be a secret in the mud. Yes. Be the worm, in one piece or two.

That's how you survive, you skip.

Kiki spun and saw me, watched as I scuttled over collapsed trees, bark like moist cardboard. My feet schlepped through upturned land, knees jarring where the ground was solid enough to carry my weight. Adrenalin shifted into overdrive—there was only a little pain, mostly behind my eyes and in my ears. Kiki tried to climb the slope. I narrowed the distance between us.

Actually, turn back, Coach said. The pivot was so like him. He'd shout conflicting advice from courtside all the time. It used to drive me mad. *If you reach her, you'll wake up. This can't be real. People don't survive something like this. You're dead, you just don't know it yet. Soon as you touch her, she won't exist anymore.*

The only way to keep her alive is to never see her again.

Kiki fell into my arms. I held her beaten face as we pressed our foreheads together. Tears carved lines through the grit on her cheeks. I cried, too. She looked down at the wood sticking out of my side. I kissed her, she kissed me. I told her I was sorry. She said she was sorry, too. I rubbed her head. She rubbed mine. We let each other know we had survived.

"Do it," I said, glancing down at the wood jutting from my flesh, and gripped Kiki's shoulder, ready to instruct her again and again until she saw that the pain trade-off would be worth it in the end. I didn't get a chance. Kiki grabbed the branch. Yanked it free. I doubled over and vomited. My head spun, so I spun with it and found myself on my back. Kiki pressed cold wet mud against my wound. "Fuck," I said. "Fuck fuck fuck."

My eyes drifted past her head to the sky. Clouds moved fast up here. That's how high we were. The sun swelled with each pound of blood, ballooning outwards, almost close enough to touch. I imagined the great ball of fire exploding us to ash, the ground turning to glass beneath us, the remains of who we used to be swirling in the wind.

16

Coach had never not been tall. Even though we were the same height by the time I was done with tennis, he remained this gigantic planet of a person to me—spinning too fast, as if outrunning the sun. His gravitational pull swept me along. No wonder it was hard, and took so long, for me to tell him what I needed. For now, he had me under his thumb. And I was tired. Tired of pushing myself. Tired of him telling me who I had to be. Tired of everything.

"The skip's got no backbone," he said, leaning over, into me, as I lay sprawled on the sandy tennis court. He often spoke as if he were talking to someone else. Someone who wasn't there. "Oi, look at me. Look me in the eye. Play like something's been stolen from you, that's what I tell him. You skips are all the same."

Coach didn't know I saw my dead brother every time the ball hit my racquet. Spliced in like the wrong frame into the wrong film. There. Not there. There. Not there.

I was tired of that, too.

15

The landslide ate my backpack, but Kiki still had hers. We huddled together, patching ourselves up as best we could with what resources we had, giving ourselves a moment to deal with the shock. We spoke in clipped sentences, testing each other to gauge if we were fit enough to function. Ha. Like we had a choice.

"It's not much," she said, voice hoarse.

We took inventory. Two baked taro cakes wrapped in alfoil. A tin of SPAM. A packet of rice crackers. A water bottle wrapped in a Christmas tea towel. A packet of Juicy Fruit. The pocketknife her father gave her before leaving Perth, her initials engraved in the side. A light scarf to shield herself from the sun. A Freemantle

Football Club beach towel. DEET mosquito repellent in an orange bottle. The crumbs of past, better meals.

"We may not need much," I said.

Her eyes fixed on mine, face etched with worry. Who could blame her?

"We'll be found, Kiki. We'll be okay. I promise you."

We packed the bag together. Kiki's movements were methodical, almost graceful, undermined by the quivering of her hands, by the blood flowering through her makeshift bandages. She was on her knees, dripping sweat. I wasn't faring much better. The sun shrank our shadows into pools we couldn't climb into.

"Time to get moving," I said. "Let's go lengthwise against the incline, stick to the shade where we can, crisscrossing higher as we go, like a Z all the way up to the crater's edge. Or what's left of it anyway."

"But it won't be stable at the top. It won't hold. It—"

"We don't have to go all the way," I said, taking her forearm. "But we need to be viewable from the sky. Nobody's going to find us down here in the scrub. We're not going into the basin. No way."

Kiki nodded: jolted up and then down too fast. Too desperate. Her lips shook. She pushed the knots of muddy hair out of her eyes, fingers coming away brown, and stood.

"And we've only got your phone now," I said. "Mine was in my backpack."

"The screens cracked to shit but it's still working at least."

"No reception?"

"Nope," Kiki said. "It comes and goes, even on this part of the island on a good day. I'll watch it like a hawk."

"Good." I wanted her to know we'd only get through this if we got through it together. "Are you ready?" I stood by her side, swinging the backpack onto my shoulders. Pain that time. If I moved too abruptly, parts of me that should not open would open again. The climb ahead: like walking a tightrope. Only there was no other way.

"Wait, Dan." Kiki peered at me from beneath her brow, the sunlight casting her eyes into black. "Pray with me."

I exhaled. "Kiki, I told you we're going to be fine."

"Not for us," she said.

Seeing her so broken hurt more than the cuts and the bruises and the wound beneath the dry earth on my side. Kiki gestured at the wall of jungle separating us from the destroyed village on the other side. We had been different people over there.

The man in his lavalava singing in an empty bar. The group by the beach who laughed and consoled me in the dark.

Nothing lasted. Everything could be broken. We were shaped to be abused whether we deserved it or not. Virtue didn't come into it at all. These were the conclusions I'd come to; my mirror. I stared at Kiki, but it wasn't her face staring back. I saw the wave and its death mask, the blue baby rising through froth with eyes that would never see. The old woman with the cracked head. I saw them all.

"Okay," I said, letting her take my hands. I kissed her dirty knuckles. "Okay, babe."

14

"What the fuck were you thinking out there?" Coach yelled, crossing the car park to where my parents were loading me into a different car, a blue car, one with a different shape and feel to the one my brother died in. My parents hardly flinched when Coach slapped me across the back of the head. Mum maybe a little. Coach shooshed her. He always did.

"This is how we get him strong," the tall man said. "How we get him to not give up like he did out there on the courts today."

Mum looked at Dad as if seeking a reason to fight this. She found nothing in his face. She glanced at Coach's large hands, noted the callouses and the wedding ring he still wore, and walked away.

That was the day I learned how much harder I was than my parents. They were soft things. Blurry things. Doughy people who no longer liked music, and who never sang together to songs like Paradise by the Dashboard Light. *I didn't use that hardness against them for a couple more years yet. It brewed. Maybe they sensed it. But if they did, there was no fight to keep me.*

13

Staccato light through the canopy as we trudged along, enormous branches rolling by. It was like glancing up from under an ocean rip curl. We're down here beneath the trees. We're drowning. We needed to be up there, far away.

Chase the sun.

We stopped for a drink of water. Little sips from the bottle. My fingers were engorged with blood and hurt to clench. We forced each other to eat some taro. It was over-salted and left me thirsty again. Kiki checked her phone.

"We've been walking for two hours," she said.

"Good."

I had informed our team leader of our trip before leaving— basic protocol many volunteers didn't see as important. I was (more or less) a stickler for the rules, despite the ribbing I copped from my housemates. Toeing the party line paid off. The Australian embassy would have already deployed a rescue team to find us by now, a privilege not awarded to the locals. Guilt wormed inside me. A very white, ugly guilt.

We pushed on, Kiki taking the lead and carrying the bag. Ten minutes ground by without us saying a word. We strode out of the trees, back into the open. The inner cusp of Mount Foliga was a busted face bleeding soil and stone, rows of shattered tree teeth that speared in every direction. Kiki stopped and looked back at me.

"Christ, Dan. Look."

There was a path marked with white stones and mossy coconut husks further up the incline, beyond the landslide scars. Even more promising, it ran along the mountain at a slight but noticeable gradient. There was no way to tell where it led, but that didn't matter. It led *somewhere*. And somewhere always led to *someone*.

"Yes, yes, yes," I said, clenching my fist. "Let's—"

A boulder shifted loose of the deadfall up the slope.

"Watch out!" Kiki shouted.

We ran up the path as the enormous rock rolled in our direction. It flattened the footprints we'd left in the unsteady soil moments before and bounced through a wall of vegetation on the other side. Our chests rose and fell in unison, breaths wheezy. We listened to the boulder's inevitable end in the crater below. Birds took flight and screeched all around us, sprinkling us in scat.

I turned to Kiki, now on her haunches, head in hand. I swallowed dry. Another brush with death. I wanted to wallow in what had almost happened, if only for a minute, and feel sorry for ourselves, seek someone to blame—anyone, everything. Only Kiki read the self-pity in my face and silenced me.

"Don't," she said, trying not to cry. "I just *can't.*"

"But aren't you scared?" I said, voice breaking. "We almost fucking died just then. Again!"

"Please be quiet, Dan," Kiki said. "Please."

"Jesus Christ, talk to me." Adrenalin kicked in. "*This is insane!*" I shouted loud enough for my voice to echo back from the jungle. I sounded unhinged.

"You think I don't know that?" she said. Kiki rocked on her haunches. "Yes, okay! Fine! This whole situation is completely fucked. The absolute worst thing that could happen. We should be dead. We should be ripped up, crushed, or buried alive. We should be those things and probably more. But we're not. Okay? We're not. Does that make you feel better, Dan, hearing me say all that?"

"Maybe it does."

"Then I'm glad to have been helpful. And now I've given you what you wanted, I just want you to be quiet and not shout and not speak and let me sit here and process."

"Come on, don't be like that, babe."

"Don't—" Kiki held her tongue. Shifted gears. Studied the sky. "Pity is only going to slow us down."

She was going to say don't call me babe anymore.

Kiki remained in her crouched position. Flies swarmed about us, landing in our blood. My pulse ebbed back into its normal rhythm. She was right. We could feel sorry for ourselves, and grateful for the slivers of luck awarded us, later. Kiki started up the path again. Stopped.

"I'm sorry, Dan," she said. "Sorry for everything."

The hurt was real. I tried to swallow but my throat felt bruised. "Me too. I feel like I made you come here when I knew you didn't want to. And look what's happened."

"I *did* want to come," she said. "I'm just confused, okay? You confuse me. We had no way of knowing all this would happen. Let's not think that way."

"I didn't mean to push you. I can be an arsehole sometimes. Fuck!"

Kiki exhaled, touched her neck, searched for the right thing to say. If such a thing existed. "We're good people who've forgotten how to be good to each other, Dan. It happens."

"Are we, though?"

"Are we what?"

"Good? Samoa doesn't need us. From day one, you called bullshit."

"I don't think that's for us to decide anymore," Kiki said. "On both counts. And look. I don't resent you for being a dude with a savior complex. Who also needs saving. It is what it is. You don't have to tell me everything about why you're really here. We can just agree to do our best with what we've got. Yeah?"

"We can try for that," I said.

"And when we're back, let's talk things through."

Tell her the truth, Coach whispered in my ear. *Tell her you killed your brother. Tell her that running is all you're good at. Tell her that you're a parasite. That you need to make yourself feel better by helping others, and when things start to get steady, start to get good, you look for ways to sabotage things. You did that with her. You pushed her away. And you did this because chaos is normal to you. Calm is threatening. Tell her. Tell it all.*

(No.)

"Okay," I said, nodding. "Okay."

I let her lead the way.

Another hour passed.

Walking on even ground eased the pain in my ankles after all the side-stepping. I offered my hand to Kiki. She took it without speaking. We continued that way for a while. Our palms slickened with sweat and we drew apart.

Crunching footfalls over hard-packed earth.

The drone of a billion insects.

Kiki asked me to turn away when she crouched to pee. I did the same thing further along. More food was nibbled at. Another sip of water. We trudged through several seasons. Summer heat. Rain with intense humidity on its heels. And then a cold mist that left us shivering before it blew away. Mosquitoes swarmed in and we reapplied the repellent we'd sweated off, but not before being bitten. And bitten. And bitten. Hands slapped skins. Welts on welts. Words like Dengue and Malaria and Zika dashed through my mind, words I cross-checked with vaccinations I'd had in the lead up to deployment.

You'll be fine. Don't worry.

Just. Keep. Walking.

Don't let Kiki see how scared you are. Not again. Never again.

The canopy peeled away behind us. We entered another clearing. I shielded my eyes from the glare. Up ahead, the path climbed the mountain at a severe angle. My sigh was definitive. This was going to hurt. But I was lucky to feel such pain. People were dead on the other side of the mountain. This island, which I loved, wasn't the same place it had been at the prior dusk, when the elders along the coast stepped from their houses in hi-vis jackets to blow their conch shells, signifying the beginning of Sa, the daily religious curfew that had to be observed by all. We'd been driving from the trench to the faleo'o huts at the time, and like other cars on the road, pulled over until the hour passed. Yes, everything and every place was different. Samoa would be grieving.

The lucky ones hurt, Dan, Coach said. *And don't you forget it.*

"Want me to take the backpack for a while?" I said. Kiki nodded and handed it over. It was still damp from the rain, or maybe perspiration. I didn't care. The straps cut into my tender shoulders. I forged ahead, knees cracking. My side was giving me hell, but I tried not to let it show. Blood trickled through a crack in the mud bandage and ran down my leg.

Kiki followed close behind.

This path is leading somewhere, I told myself. *And we're heading in the right direction, sort of. We'll come to a village soon enough. The locals won't be that accustomed to palangi dropping in. We'll be welcomed. They'll feed us taro leaves stewed in coconut cream, cooked just right so the poison won't sting out throats. We'll be brought before the chief who'll delegate a crew to take us over the mountain in one of their trucks. We might even end up spending the night. Kiki and I will weave mats with the women if they want our help, and drink beer from long-necked bottles with the men. There will be a fire. Cold water to wash in. They'll see to our wounds. And at the end of all this, they will pray and cry for us, and for those who hadn't reached the mountain in time, those crushed and beaten to death by the Pacific. Pray the pain away.*

"Dan, look," Kiki said. She pointed. I tilted my head, saw the mountain and its path, a V of rock sixty yards above.

We were no longer alone.

Someone stood in the V. A silhouette against the blue sky.

You can breathe again, Dan.

"Oh, thank fuck," I said. "We did it."

She waved her arms and shouted greetings in the native tongue. I did the same. "He can see us, right?"

I wanted to answer yes, but I couldn't be sure. The figure hadn't moved or signaled back. Unease prickled through me, trying to spear up through the skin. Goosebumps on goosebumps.

Perhaps we'd jumped the gun and mistaken an *actual* statue for a man or woman. But not even that made sense. This wasn't Rome or Greece. You would be hard pressed to find David-esque renderings of chiseled masculinity anywhere in this country. Come to think of it, the only statues I'd seen in Samoa were of Christ with his crown of thorns, concrete eyes always open and always watching.

This silhouette raised their hands.

I half-laughed. Kiki sighed. She must have felt it, too. The unease. "He's seen us," I said. "Come on, let's—"

The figure clapped five times, each retort like rocks being snapped together. *Clack! Clack! Clack! Clack! Clack!* Echoes through the basin. Fading, fading. The figure withdrew from sight and slipped beyond the V of stone. The blue sky left behind was an invitation we couldn't ignore.

"Tag, you're it," I said, taking the bait, turning to give Kiki a wink. "Here we go."

12.

Trophies on the windowsill: cheap figures of men and boys holding tennis racquets, lined up next to candles set on tea plates, the wax burned down to hardened pools. Dust on my fingertips when I touched the toy faces, mementos of wins, the guys I'd thrashed on courts of clay and sand. These days, all Coach spoke about were the upcoming Olympics. This roughly translated to: Get ready for a world of pain, kid. *I knew about pain already. My body was changing and ached with growth. I'd showed my* trophies to a girl in my room that night. Her name was Stef and she said she liked me, even though she thought I was sad all the time, even when I laughed.

Tissues on the floor. A damp towel. Two condoms in the garbage can under my desk tied into knots so the cum didn't dribble out. We thought we had the house to ourselves for a few more hours. We found out how wrong we were within minutes.

My parents caught Stef climbing into her clothes and escorted her out of the house. I wished Mum and Dad yelled at me. Silence was worse. They didn't know how to love anymore—not themselves, each other, or me. Grief was all they knew. The only way I could exist with them was for Cory to have never existed. That ultimatum proved too much to take. I told them to get fucked and ran away from home, spitting at their doorstep before heading into the night. I wore my tennis shoes. They squeaked as I ran. Light rain fell in sheets.

I banged on Coach's door twelves blocks away.

He answered after a short while. Coach had no wife. She died before Mum and Dad asked him to steer me away from trouble, after the accident. Give him discipline, I recalled them saying. He needs it. Maybe they wanted me out of the way. They had no reason to blame me, didn't know what I'd done, the secret guilt I carried. Survival was enough. There were days I wish I hadn't lived. To some degree, they manifested my shitty attitude. Provoked me. Taunted me. All with the purpose of justifying how they pushed me into Coach's life. I didn't know I was bad until they told me I was bad. And when I succeeded on the courts, my parents had the nerve to take credit for setting me on this path. They knew they could get away with it at the time because I was a kid. Well, I wasn't a kid anymore. I could legally move out in three months. Was grown enough, man enough, to make Stef feel like a woman. She told me that, said those very words, before Mum and Dad came home. It almost made me cry. I didn't, though. I hadn't cried since Cory's funeral.

That was about to change.

Coach stood on the doorstep in boxer shorts and a white t-shirt. Moths swarmed about us. I made to enter but he held me at arm's length. I told him what happened.

"Oi, look at me. Look me in the eye. Go home." His words were brutish, but he sounded tender as I'd ever heard him. "I don't care what they said to you, Dan. Why would I parent you when your folks can do it for you? I coach because I get paid. If you want to rock up at my doorstep at sparrow's fart, come back with a check. Go home and show respect to your mum and dad, even if they don't respect you. That's how you win the game. You hear me? You understand me?"

He noted the tears on my cheeks. Softened.

The rain kept coming down.

"Come back when you're eighteen," he said, and closed the door.

I went home, hugging myself all the way.

My parents' house (it hadn't been mine in years) looked like an uncaring face. I wanted to punch myself in the head for opening the screen door, punch myself again for walking down the hall, punch myself again for passing their room where I knew Mum and Dad weren't asleep, where they had been waiting for me to come back, and punch myself again for entering my bedroom where things had been so good so short a time ago. The trophies watched me not punch myself as I turned off the lamp and slipped beneath the covers. An hour passed, maybe more, maybe less. Tossed. Turned. I sensed my brother in the room with his gouged off face and glass shard eyes. I could hear him gurgling my name through the puckered hole where his mouth used to be. Waited for the pop of his blood bubble. Cory was here but couldn't cross over. Something barred the way. A kind of veil. I hoped it was a hug he wanted to give me. I feared revenge above all else.

11

It didn't require a well-trained tracker to pinpoint the footprints in the mud between the rocks where the figure had stood, and note the direction they led. Our friend was flatfooted. Heavier than they appeared, perhaps. And whoever they were, they went—

"This way," I said, gesturing to yet another grove of trees on our right, the path marked by the same painted coconuts and stones. We limped on.

Butterflies jittered in beams of light spearing the enmeshed branches. The crunch of earth under our sodden shoes. Kiki and I had been through a lot, and our journey was far from over. There was a strong possibility the Corps would send us back to Australia for a full psychological evaluation, and ground us for good. It had happened to other volunteers for far less. It occurred to me then that I was already mourning. I just wasn't done with Samoa yet. No, not by a long shot. And if I were to leave, I wished to do so on my own terms. I was confident Kiki felt the same way. Not that we mentioned it as we walked through that still air, with the sounds of crunching earth in our ears. To do so would jinx us, and we'd been through enough already. A butterfly landed on my arm. Tickle-tickle. Large wings came together like hands playing peekaboo, and flapped with a soft *pat-pat-pat* as it took off. We followed the butterflies, guided by them. Closer now to whatever came next.

Stone struck stone again further around the bend, just out of sight.

Clack! Clack! Clack! Clack! Clack!

"Let's go," Kiki said, taking the lead. She didn't wait.

We emerged into a patch of long-ago smoothed land marking entry to a village on the crater's slope. The sight of these buildings almost brought me to my knees. Combined, too, with the whirring of a distant helicopter.

Kiki spun, her eyes wide. She ran to me, arms slipping around my shoulders. We jumped up and down, even though it must have hurt her as much as it hurt me. Her cheek pressed against mine. I didn't care if I bled anymore.

"We did it," she said. "We're gonna be okay!"

"I told you! Can you see the chopper?"

We drew apart, hands still on each other's wrists, and tilted our chins to the sky. Clouds skimmed the crater's edge. The sun blinked through, spitting warmth on our faces. Those helicopter blades continued to thump somewhere, growing louder and dimmer at the same time. A combination of distance and wind, maybe. Neither of us saw the rescue team. No matter. We weren't imagining things. Help was on the way.

"How do we signal to them?" Kiki said.

"We'll call the office from here. Someone will have a phone. Wait, check yours for reception. We might be in luck."

"Oh, Dan, we did it," Kiki said, drawing out her mobile. She clucked her tongue. "Still nothing. Surprise surprise."

"It doesn't matter anymore."

Kiki lifted her soiled, bruised hands to her face. The emotion there was messy and raw. "I was so worried."

I rubbed her back. It stung when she wriggled free of my touch. It wasn't a conclusive gesture, not completely—*I'll be fine* minus the words. I let her go. Kiki drew a deep breath. I was too excited to be disappointed.

"Where is everyone?" she said.

"Well, what time is it?" I wondered if it was six o'clock. Sa might be underway. That, at least, would explain why nobody was outside. Kiki drew out her phone again and checked. To our shock, it was only just after three. The hours had contracted and flexed a dozen times over, minutes sometimes rushing by only to crawl a moment later. I listened for noise. Any noise. There were no sounds of children at play. No tell-tale reggae beat of off-season Christmas carols. No conch shell being blown. Nothing but the hiss of the jungle, the rumble of wind over our sunburned ears.

"No dogs, either," Kiki said. "No animals at all."

She was right. No bird song. Even the butterflies, silent as they were, hadn't crossed into the village, instead looping back into the trees to dance in the light beams.

"It's abandoned," Kiki said, disheartened.

"It can't be, though. We saw someone. They waved us in." I took a second to compose myself. Forced a smile. "Look, even if the place *is* abandoned, it doesn't matter all that much to us. We're close to the crater's edge now. Where there's a town there'll be a path or road up over the top and down the other side to the coast. And even then, the helicopters are near enough to probably spot us, and—"

As if listening, the whine of the emergency crew began to recede.

Mist and shadow kissed the old brown buildings with their empty windows, howled through a large open-floor fale, its palm leaf roof ripped to shreds. A shutter clattered on its hinge somewhere, the sound a lonely *knock-knock-knock*.

I took a few steps. Winced. Skin tight over my wound.

"Dan—"

"It's fine," I said, even if I didn't believe things were fine. "Come on."

Nine structures comprised the village; slanting buildings made of cement and cinderblock, wooden doors and tattered netting, coconut husks and barbed wire. I stepped into the nearest home, my shadow spilling across the floor where cockroaches scuttled back and forth. An old bucket sat in the corner of the single room, next to the remains of a long-dead chicken. The far wall was decorated with a life-sized drawing of a sexless human rendered in chalk-like paint. I was reminded of corpse outlines at murder sites in the police procedural shows I used to watch with Coach ("I know who did it," he would always say, clicking his fingers at the screen—even though he was always wrong). This outline had been filled in. The artist stayed within the lines, like something a child might do. Only, no. This wasn't a rush job. The artist had a careful hand, the kind of hand that carefully wove matts, or plaited hair, whittled wood. Methodical work. Almost respectful. Reverent.

Asking if anyone was home would have been redundant.

The place was empty, and the painting on the wall wasn't going to offer any answers, either. I sighed, lingering on the chicken carcass for a few seconds before trudging back to the muddy street with Kiki. We scratched our heads. The sun beamed bright on us, throwing our shadows across the ground. There was another unmistakable shadow near us, too.

A crucifix.

I looked to the church ahead, the largest building in the village. No songs could be heard over the howling wind. I figured there *might* be a chance the town's whole population—so much as it was—could be within those walls. A ceremony underway, perhaps. Or a funeral. Only it would be unlike any Samoan funeral I'd witnessed. Grief was bright and loud here—so different from the pearl-clutching back home. And then, when the body was released, the loved one would be buried in the family's front yard. Graves marked with round stones. There were three graves within the boundaries of our compound in Apia. I often wondered who these people were, what they did and how they'd died. It was comforting, not frightening, seeing these markers so close to the house. Death wasn't hidden in Samoa. I envied that. How different things might have been out for me if I hadn't lived with people who would rather pretend they'd never had another son than acknowledge their hurt. Loss doesn't evaporate into steam you walk through. You just get more adept at managing the symptoms. I had my own ways of dealing, ways that were quiet and grotesquely western. Private ways. Those coping strategies—sex, for example, relationship hopping—were bad enough. Mum and Dad, meanwhile, managed their grief by pretending they had nothing to be damaged by. I hated my parents for that.

No wonder I kept running.

10

I readied myself to go back to Coach on my eighteenth birthday, just like he told me to. The prior three months had been spent seething in my room. In the end, Mum and Dad begged me not to leave. Their desperation caught me off guard. I'd expected them to be numb. I wasn't so lucky. They tore at my clothes as they pulled me back into the house and threw me into my room again. The door was locked behind me. I escaped through the window.

The tarmac under my feet as I ran.

No knocking on Coach's door this time. I strode on in with a bag under my arm.

I found him in his living room sipping a beer on the couch, feet up in front of the television with the Greek news blasting on SBS. He stormed at me again, but I held my ground. We stared at each other. He probably expected me to cower. I didn't. Men like Coach didn't respect those who did. The room shrunk with the two of us in it, squaring off, face to face. I felt in charge, at least for a moment, the ball in his court.

Deuce.

"Happy birthday," he said. And handed me his beer.

9

I approached the church, passing another building on my left, another chalk drawing on its outer wall. The figure's arms and legs were mid-dance, pantomiming life. A chill ran through me, despite the afternoon heat.

My boots clumped against the single step leading into the church, which was empty, as suspected. My disappointment filled the open space, seeped between the weaves of the hand-crafted mats on the floor, bounced off the makeshift altar. The only thing that signified this room as a place of worship was an old painting of a tortured Christ that had fallen off its hook and now rested sideways on the floor.

"It's all so uncanny, don't you reckon?" Kiki said behind me.

I flinched, on edge.

"And look."

She had her phone out and was clicking photographs of the chalk figures lining the mossy walls. Some of these figures stood alone, arms crooked at wrong angles and heads disproportionately sized to their bodies. Others were hand in hand, like a chain of paper dolls strung across the door of one of the kindergarten classes she'd supervised in Savai'i.

"Don't take too many pictures," I said. "You'll kill your battery. We might need your phone after all."

"Not much good it's doing us, anyway."

"You never know."

Kiki pocketed her mobile and put her hands on her hips. "This place sure would make a good art series, I guess. Graffitiville. That's what we'd call it." She hugged herself. "Let's get out of here, Dan. I feel like someone just walked over my grave."

"What about the person who led us here?" I said. "We know there's people—"

"And they don't want to be seen. Let's respect that."

8

Coach would sooner cut off his hand than have a freeloader in his house. I paid rent on that spare room, sleeping on a hard bed surrounded by piles of tax records from numerous failed businesses. I scrounged through his mess for the fun of it. Old bills. Return to Sender mail he'd never dropped back off at the post office. One time, I found a stack of gay magazines full of naked models, cocks of every size poking in every direction. I slipped them back where I found them, ashamed for having snooped where I shouldn't have.

Sometimes, I heard Coach talking to my parents on the phone from the other room.

Words like: "He is fine" and "I'll let you know" and "Sure".

It helped if I thought they were talking about Cory.

He's (not) fine. I'll let you know if he's (not) dead.
Sure, he's coming home one day.
(Not.)
Coach only slapped the back of my head one more time, on the night he caught me sneaking a girl out of his house. The door was heavy. Its lock a gnashing of teeth. I found him in the hall behind me.
"Suppose you think you're clever," he said.
"You're not my Dad."
"Malaka."
"Don't talk to me like that. You're a cunt, that's all you are," I said, stepping by him. That was when he slapped me. I swear I felt my brain rattle inside my skull.
"Big talk from a little guy. Want me to increase your rent? Hard to focus on getting to the Olympics if you knock up some girl. Don't you see I'm trying to keep you on track? You're right. I'm not your mum or your pin-dick papa. I give a shit."
"You got a funny way of showing it then. I don't have to put up with this, you know."
"Then don't put up with it," Coach said. "Keep running. That's all you skips do. Oi, look at me. Look me in the eye. That's right. Run and run and run, rabbit."
I expected him to push on with his tirade, and in many ways, I wished he had. I could have volleyed with him for longer. Instead, he returned to his room and closed the door. With nobody to be angry at and nowhere else to go, I went to my room and picked up my racquet and a few tennis balls I slipped into the pockets of my shorts. Coach's door opened again when I stepped onto the veranda.
"Where you going? It's the middle of the night. Get back inside."
"I'll be back," I said. Paused. Exhaled. "Look, I'm sorry, okay."
He didn't reply, just watched me go. I walked through the night to the high school around the corner and pounded the tennis ball against the back brick wall until sweat coursed my face and chest. Every thrash, every thwack of rubber against gut-wire, burned the anger out of me. Bit by bit. Soon, I sat on the ground. Studied the sky.
This was where I came to when things got tough. This was what I did. I put my hurt into the ball and then punished the ball.

Some nights, I thought I saw someone moving in the dark. It was hard to see this person if you looked where you expected them to be. They hovered in your periphery. On the edges. Between all places with the glimmer of wet glass where their eyes should be.

7

Kiki was about to walk out of the church, but stopped at the threshold. I'd been busy studying the wall art when she gasped, took half a step back.

"What?" I said, stopping next to her, warm sunshine on my face.

"Shhh."

She pointed to a naked figure in the middle of the muddy strip we'd walked down.

This was the man, or maybe it was a boy, who had signaled to us from the V of rock on the path. Or at least, I assumed this person was male. It was difficult to tell.

One thing was certain, though.

Their skin was painted white from head to toe.

I strode out into the street, leaving Kiki framed by the dark mouth of the church.

"Don't, Dan!" she whisper-yelled.

I had no intention of chasing the kid down for answers, or of being aggressive. I only wanted to ask if they could help us. I didn't get a chance.

The boy raised his hands once again. Struck his palms together, plumes of white dust clouding the air.

Clack! Clack! Clack! Clack! Clack!

I glanced to Kiki in the doorway. She wasn't alone.

A white shape emerged from the darkness behind her.

"KIKI!" I screamed, rushing towards her as the figure thudded the back of her head with a clenched fist. She hit the uneven steps face-first. Teeth shattered. A splash of blood. Shock clenched me from within, drawing my focus into an iris. The attacker dragged Kiki backwards into the church. Air thickened. Time slowed. I stepped over tooth fragments and through the archway, shouting Kiki's name as though it were an invocation, something I could weaponize. I was scared, yes. But angry, too. There was no racquet

and ball for me to take that anger out on. No way to bleed it free. So, I took that anger into the church. I would no longer run. I was a tsunami. My anger wore the faces of every person who had wronged me. Their eyes were wide, mouths gumming screams. My fists rose. I knuckled the dim light. Evening fell swiftly in Samoa.

It took a moment for my eyes to adjust. Kiki was on the floor next to the altar. A tall man painted in white crouched over her. He lifted his head. The man had no face. Bald, clayish. A dried riverbed come to life.

We'd been alone in the church together—of that, I was sure. This was impossible. There had been nowhere for this guy to hide. Yet here he was.

My heart trip-hammered at the abrupt sound of rock hitting rock on my right. I spun, disorientated, and watched one of the chalk paintings pry itself off the wall, stepping into reality a leg at a time. The man who had struck Kiki, just like the kid outside, was not covered in paint. If only that had been so. They *were* paint.

"The fuck—" was about as far as I got before the figure's overlong arm reached from the wall towards me, rocky fingers curling upwards in invitation.

A flicker of shadow over the floor. Someone behind me.

Pain detonated in the middle of my back. I fell forward, cushioning the fall with the heels of my palms, the old woven mat disintegrating into strands under the force. Grit shot up my nose, into my eyes. The scuttle of rocky feet—they sounded like hooves. I tried to roll onto my side but the person (or was it a thing?) that struck me swooped low once again.

6

I was twenty-two and had given up professional tennis, happier to be pushing trolleys at the local Woolworths. At that point in my life, ambition frightened me more than men's singles opponents. I was chipping away at a TAFE course in community development. The walls of my little room at Coach's house were plastered in cutouts from magazines I'd cribbed from the office of the psychologist I sometimes saw at Coach's insistence. These tearaways featured all the places I wanted to visit.

Samoa was in the mix.

Friday.

A cold evening.

I came home after my shift, phone beeping with a reminder from Dad to call Mum for her birthday the following morning. We were at least talking a little these days. If talk was what you could call it. We corresponded. My key stuck in the jam during the winter months, so it always took a bit of force to get in the house. The old door dropped as it swung, glow from the veranda light slicing along the hall to illuminate Coach's body on the carpet. He was face up with the landline gripped in one hand. I dropped to my knees beside him and tried to breathe life into his lungs through the gap in his thick Greek lips. That mouth had been so quick to insult and hurt me over the years, but it had also ensured I was seen. And heard. I hated that I'd disappointed him by stepping away from the game. I hated myself for ever clapping back at him. I hated it all.

"Don't do this, you bastard!" I screamed, thumping his chest. "You can't!"

Coach's face was cold when I kissed him goodbye. Dewy lips. He'd showered before his heart gave out. He smelled of his good hair oil and cologne. Maybe he'd been intending to go and meet someone. That person might have looked like his wife. Perhaps they weren't a woman at all. I didn't know. I didn't need to know. I only wished love for him someday from someone kind.

Things untethered. It felt like I was lifting into the air, floating through the ceiling and into the sky, burning like a meteorite in reverse as I spun into space. Coach had outrun the sun for so long. Now the pursuit was over.

At some point, I took out my mobile phone and called Dad. He arrived as the ambulance pulled up outside.

5

I woke bound wrist to ankle.

The chalk figures dragged me across grass on a vine hammock. They sparked dusty clouds when their limbs scraped together. No language I could hear or looks I could see were exchanged between them, yet they worked in unison, as if this were something they had done many times over. Like ants. I caught glimmers of the pink sky above, here and there through the branches of the trees they pulled me between, those enormous flowers resembling sad faces. The jungle reeked of rot and honey.

Blood in my mouth. Only the mosquitoes made noise. They fed on me. I craned my head to see where I was being taken, and to my surprise saw Kiki, also bound and bleeding, led by the chalk figures through a lightning bolt-shaped part in the foliage. She screamed. I watched her try to pull away as a rocky hand thudded her into submission. I begged for the both of us, but my throat was dry.

Canopy swallowed pink sky.

Mosquitoes dug their needles deeper. Pain roiled inside my skin, cracking up through my chest and into my shoulders, my side, in the middle of my head and behind my eyes. I tried to wiggle my fingers. Just numbness below the wrist. They had tied me tight.

Leaves whipped my face as they dragged us further into the scrub.

I, too, attempted to roll away and make an escape for it. One of the chalk figures knocked me back into place. Dull pain. Breathing came hard.

We were dragged into a clearing before the crater wall, a place where grass didn't grow. They threw Kiki at the foot of an enormous, silvery lattice. A great tree must have stood at that spot for hundreds, maybe thousands of years before being strangled by an invasive species of vine. Over time, the tree died, mulched by weather until all that remained was the murder vine itself. It had calcified. And now glowed in the dusk. Wind blew through its honeycombed bulk, a choir of whistles. Power beamed off its girth like the burning of ozone before a storm.

My body jolted. Kangaroo in headlights fear. Nerves crunching like metal and glass.

Kiki struggled. The jungle echoed her shrieks. Or taunted her. Mocking. For the first time since entering the village—*Graffitiville*, Kiki had named it—there were bird calls and crying insects. Noise everywhere; a roar that came on cue. Except for the chalk people who had no eyes to see with (yet saw) and who had no mouths to command with (yet whose instructions couldn't be denied). One of them smacked Kiki across the back of the neck again. A casual flick of the wrist with the impact of a tossed brick. I felt that crunch in my own body. Kiki toppled to the ground before the lattice tree. I hoped she would pass out. Neither of us were so lucky.

99

"No," I managed to get out. Maybe I should have said 'love'.

A chalk figure took a step towards me. I winced at the blow to come should I dare speak again. The figure grabbed the sides of my head, locked me in place, its grip a vice. The message was clear: I had been brought here to watch. If I didn't comply, it would burst my skull.

Kiki pulled at her restraints, but her captors weren't in the mercy-giving mood. One pinned her down while the other rounded her from behind and grabbed her foot. Chalky fingers splashed red as it yanked the Achilles Heel from her ankle with the casual indifference of someone drawing weeds from a garden. I screeched. Watched the blood gush. Kiki fought. She didn't stand a chance. The figure grabbed her other ankle and stripped her of those strings, too. A tuft of gore was thrown at the lattice. The two chalk figures scuttled to their feet on mismatched legs, and monkey-walked over to me. Kiki was alone now and unable to move.

She squirmed, flung her head my way. Her eyes through knots of bloodied hair. I wished the tsunami had claimed us after all. That we hadn't run so fast. Or climbed so high.

Leeches seeped out of the dirt and latched to my legs, fattening on my fluids. It seemed only fair that those who use and feed on others are fed on and used in the end. Did guilt sweeten or sour the taste of blood? Leeches probably didn't care. They only hungered.

Kiki kept her eyes on me. I willed her to never stop seeking me out. Ever. No matter what happened next.

A shadow passed behind the ancient lattice. Something *big*. It descended with acrobatic ease, swirling down its length, making a drumming sound as it moved.

The chalk figures didn't react.

Piss flooded my crotch.

Mosquitoes hazed the air.

Wind blew through the lattice and the roadkill stench of dead things rolled over us.

A creature spindled from the base of the lattice, incisors clipping like garden shears. Kiki closed her eyes. The mammoth centipede flipped right side up, flexing multi-jointed legs, and snatched her up by the head. Brains fanned the hardpacked earth. Antennae twitched, whipping blood and ribbons of flesh. The centipede's segments, each the size of a sewer manhole, crashed together as it curled in on itself, folding Kiki in half, her spine snapping, and dragged her away, up into the lattice of vine and shadow.

My screams ran out at some point. The grip on my head loosened. I was ready for my turn. Only the chalk figures turned their backs on their totem and pulled me up the incline instead, back to Graffitiville. Some of my leeches popped on the way. Others did not.

4

I sat at the kitchen table in my parents' house. The air was barbed. I didn't hate them the way I used to, or at least I didn't think I did. I just resented how they didn't know how to love me, that they gawked in my direction as if I were an alien, a twenty-three-year-old fetus outside its womb, and they were wondering why it was made in the first place.

"Mum?" I said. She looked up from her grey meal to reveal her grey face. "Dad?" He looked up from his grey meal to reveal his grey face.

"Yes?" they said in unison.

"I'm leaving for good," I said. "I might even try to leave the country. You can't stop me now."

They didn't even try.

3

Bound on the church floor again. A portrait of stars in a window.

Vibrations of the great wave rumbled through my aching body. I was convinced I'd never be without them now. I imagined Kiki in its waters, tumbling, seaweed in her hair. Not devoured by the monster in the clearing in the jungle. These moments of make-believe helped, but not much.

What if we hadn't set off earlier that morning?

What if we hadn't come to that part of the island earlier that week?

What if we had never come to this country at all?

What if I'd stopped pushing Kiki into distancing herself from me because the comfort and calm of what we were sharing was actually a kind of threat?

What if?

These questions had teeth.

I wormed across the floor, leaving scuff marks in the grit. No water in me at all. The evening was warm and bright. I peered around the architrave, my vision blurry from crying. Chalk figures, freed from their walls, filled the street. No voices. Just the squelch of stone against mud as they made their graceful turns and swings. Smooth heads pressed against one another, unable to kiss. They danced in the moonlight. My heart raced. It was beautiful.

Sleep dragged me under.

Dawn poked at my face until the blackness dissolved and I faded onto the concrete floor again. It was harder than I remembered, harder than any floor should be. Bones popped out of alignment under my skin. I choked when a chalk man clunked into the church.

Ear chimes. Pain flare. It was as if they had planted one of the leeches in my brain and it had grown obese on my will to live, expanding as I slept, flexing against the interior of my skull. The leech was the memory of what they had done to Kiki, of Coach dead on the floor of his home, of my brother's corpse in the rain next to the kangaroo with the backwards legs. Soon my skull would crack under the pressure.

The chalk man crouched beside me, knees scraping concrete. I flinched at the sound. It pushed a wooden bowl in my direction. I'd sensed age and power emanating from my captor, as I had with the vine tree in the clearing the night before. White sludge pooled in the bowl. The liquid stunk of earth and ammonia.

Paint, I thought. *It brought me paint?*

Confusion must have been evident in my expression. The chalk figure nudged the bowl again. The rim pressed against my thighs, slop swishing to the nimbus. Not a drop spilled.

"What?" I said, voice a croak.

The chalk man tilted its oversized head.

"I—don't—know—what—"

It swung its arm and pointed at the wall, extending a rocky finger.

Only then did I notice what the chalk figure had also brought with it. A paintbrush of coarse hair and leaves bound in twine.

"No," I said.

The chalk figure placed the brush next to the bowl and stared at me with its eyeless face. I was seen. And not in the simplistic, peripheral way. My secrets were exposed. My desires. It saw Kiki and the person I'd hoped she would become with me. It saw my family. It saw Coach. Saw Cory in his booster seat. It saw me naked and pure. And the chalk figure didn't care. It smashed its arm against the floor, fragments pinwheeling, dust exploding like dropped flour. My vision clouded. I coughed. Spat. Coughed again.

It put its handless stump to my throat, the flints sharp as razors. This creature was white and chalky through and through.

"Okay," I said. "I'll do it."

I reached for the brush. Getting a good grip proved difficult considering how numb my hands were, almost brown from a lack of circulation. But by wedging the root between my bindings, I could, with both wrists, direct the brush with enough articulation. At no point did I assume the chalk figure demanded artistry. It pushed the bowl, keeping it within reach. Splash by splash, I dove the brush into the sludge and scraped fibers against the wall. Hair over concrete. My haggard breaths as I worked. Tears on my cheeks. Paint speckled the floor as I swiped left and right, filling in the outline. Grit against grit. Strands of hair were left under the sticky mass, but the shape was clear. A head. A torso. Arms and legs.

Exhausted, I swung the brush for one final dive to mop the dregs. And froze. A human jawbone sat at the bottom of the bowl, there with shards and knuckles. A gold tooth glimmered up at me through the white broth I'd used as paint.

Kiki's diamond at the bottom of the lake.

I screamed. The leech screamed in my head, too.

My painting, like the chalk, remained silent.

2

I sat in the car I'd bought with tennis savings and trolley earnings. It wasn't that hot, but I was sweating. I'd dressed in a formal shirt and blazer over black jeans in the hopes of feigning professionalism in the interview.

"Fuck!" I said.

I sounded like him. Like Coach.

Go fix yourself, you skip. You stink like you've been on the courts all day. Wash up before you come to my table again. If you want to be a pig, expect slops.

Panting. Nervous that I'd be caught in a lie because how could I be as good a person as I'd made myself out to be in the application when that face stared back at me in the mirror? I ran into a grocery store across the road, bought a can of deodorant, slipped back into the car.

"You can do this," I told myself.

I undid the top button on my shirt and elbowed the can of deodorant in. It was only when I pushed on the circular knob—

(my fingers on my brother's seat belt)

—that I realized I'd bought shaving cream by mistake. Lather bubbled over my hairy underarm and across my chest, reaching up through the collar of my shirt like snow. Not that I'd ever seen snow. That's how narrow and small my world was. That's how badly I wanted to work for free in the hopes of finding something bigger than this.

More. I needed more.

"Fuck!"

There was a roll of toilet paper in the backseat from a camping trip the weekend before. I'd gone with a girl who broke up with me the day after. Said I was too clingy. I wanted someone to hold me. There was nobody there. I wiped off the menthol sludge, told the reflection in the rearview mirror what a fucking idiot I'd be for not telling these people all I had to offer, and buttoned up my collar. I stank of the shave. I didn't know if I could do this. Running would be easier. I held true, got out of my car and approached the building. Walked inside. Stepped into the room behind a frosted door with the words Australian Corps on the glass. Saw the man and the woman rising, their hands outstretched as they sat me at a desk and told me to take a deep breath. Because they wanted me to succeed.

1

My second quiet dusk in Graffitiville village.

The chalk figure led me, bound, from the church. I tried to steal one last look at my painting on the wall inside. Cockroaches scuttled from shadows to lick my sweat and shit and piss on the floor. The painting was still tacky to touch. I knew this because I'd put my face to it and cried an hour before. Pressed against it, hopeful the arms I'd crafted from Kiki's bone chalk paint would pry off the walls and wrap around me. Kiki's arms. That didn't happen. Nobody touched me, or rubbed my head. Nobody told me things would get better.

They led me to the tower of vine, the fight in me gone now. I screamed for Kiki, mourned her. The jungle didn't care. Trees groaned against one another. Leaves swatted the air. I'd never seen a twilight so reconciled with itself.

I tried not to think about what the chalk figures must have done after their last sacrifice—and failed. How they returned to the clearing to gather Kiki's flesh-stripped bones where the centipede spat them out. Tried not to hear how they must have clattered, hollow yet solid at once, as the chalk non-men and non-women hugged those bones close—and also failed. I didn't want to see them grinding Kiki's skeleton into dust with their pestle fists, how they tipped water from jungle leaves into the bowl and stirred until the paint coalesced.

But I did see. I saw it all.

They ripped me so I couldn't escape. I kneeled before the silvery lattice, the chalk people of Graffitiville receding into the dim. Helicopters buzzed somewhere. On the other side of the crater, rescue teams would be searching for survivors. Some of the emergency crews would be locals, but I imagined the majority would be from the surrounding islands and countries. And these strangers would bring the stink of money with them. The stink of the West. And as they had done so many times before, they would rebuild what the wave broke apart in their own image. The vine that destroys the tree becomes the tree.

I lifted my head and watched the great God centipede descend.

0

Questioner: Thanks, Dan. We've really appreciated your honesty today.

Interviewee: That's okay. I'm glad I did this. I was pretty nervous.

Questioner Two: So, what do you think?

Questioner: I think we can tell him.

Interviewee: Tell me what?

Questioner Two: You got the job, kid.

PART THREE
THE SWEEPING

"Each painful day and every hour
Break the bitch, this bastard's sour
Now you're smoke I walked right through
I burned the all worlds I walked with you."

—Dom King Come, *Our Mile*

1

There is what I used to know as dancing. But I'm not to go to where they dance. I'm devoured; not honored enough for that yet. Trees whisper how my time will come. Until then, I have much to do. So much to give. If I can make sense of whatever is The Now. I feel the memories of what came before this. Everything is out of order, the mosaic of who I used to be slipping away, piece by piece.

The centipede slinks back into its burrow, my bones piled neatly for the claiming at its base. That's who I was. The tally of me. The rustle of leaves against leaves sounds like sweeping in an empty house. Darkness has fallen in full now.

Take me to the dance, I ask the jungle. *I've earned that, haven't I?*

Sorrow drags me to the soil—if sorrow it is. These feelings are different. The wires do not connect. I wait for the rasp of chalk against chalk, stone punching mud, and then the feeling of once icy but now warm fingers cusping my cheek, lifting my chin. I wait for a kiss that doesn't come.

I hate that I can't join them in their dance under the moon.

The way is barred by figures in the trees. There are the three Samoan guys and the handsome fa'afafine I drank beers with by the bonfire. They no longer laugh, or smile. "Talofa lava," I try to say, but no sound comes out. We are not alone. Another man stands between two colossal ferns. He is tall and has thick Greek lips. I used to know him. He is full of secrets. Flowers draw apart and someone steps into the clearing. This person limps closer than he's ever been before, bringing with him the stink of blood, rain, and kangaroo piss. Little hands draw shards of glass from where his eyes used to sit. A red bubble pops.

Cory says my name.

QUICKSILVER

J.S. BREUKELAAR

HEARTSICK

1

LONG AGO, in a tiny Polish village alongside a shallow swamp, lived the boy Yoske, the only son of a poor housepainter. In those days, goats grazed in the streets and children played shoeless in the marketplace; wives emptied their piss pots, traded gossip and superstition, and the thousand-year-old oaks of the great forest cast long shadows over it all.

It was in this faraway place that fourteen-year-old Yoske wandered through the lanes of the reeking marketplace, dreaming of being somewhere else. He wanted to be a real artist, to work in rich oils and delicate watercolors instead of the house paint that stung the back of his throat. Yoske had not always been an only child. His older brother had died fighting the Cossacks, brave soldier and larrikin that he was, so the younger boy had no choice but to take up his father's profession. Dutifully he held the ladder, cleaned the brushes, white-washed fences—but truly, Yoske's heart was on the far horizon, even as his soul cried out for something he couldn't yet name.

On the boy's fifteenth birthday the old man inevitably fell to his death from the bathhouse roof where he'd been painting over some scrawled obscenity. With the grim reality of his future as a *shtetl* housepainter now before him, Yoske took final refuge in his tattered sketch book, leafing through pictures he copied from books and old newspapers—dukes and pretenders, ladies of court, pirates, tigers and rearing stallions. One day he passed the sketchbook to his friend, Lewi, to ask him what he thought of his latest drawing, a Russian frigate in a terrible storm.

"What I think," the baker's boy, Lewi, said, "is for you to join the army like your brother, may he rest in peace." He burped. "Only way out of this shithole is in a coffin, and at least in uniform you die a hero."

Crestfallen, Yoske hurled the sketchbook in a ditch. The winter that followed was long and bitter.

In spring, a traveling merchant peddling the cheap storybooks of the day happened upon the sketchbook in the ditch where it still lay, torn and wet; the artist's name smudged beyond legibility. Yet some of the drawings were intact, preserved in the innermost folds—there was, in the merchant's opinion, a boldness and sophistication to the lines that you didn't see every day. Inquiries at the village tavern led him to Yoske, halfway up a rickety ladder in the schoolhouse, mechanically slapping paint over a window frame as if in a dream. The merchant got the boy regular work with a publishing house, illustrating fairy tales and school primers, and although it wasn't very well paid, it kept Yoske and his widowed mother from the poor house. And, as Lewi the baker's boy said, at least you couldn't get shot or break your neck doing it.

A day finally came for the matchmaker to find the lad a wife. He'd grown tall and fair and had already affected the stoop and myopic gaze of the tortured artist, his only defense against the engulfing despair. Who would have him, wondered the village women, eventually settling on the orphan Ahava, a raven-haired girl who sold cookies to keep herself and her sickly twin sister from the poorhouse. The women had their work cut out trying to raise a dowry, which amounted to so little that soon after the wedding, Yoske was forced to supplement his illustration work by tutoring the children of the Christian landowners.

Yet he couldn't let go of his dream. He knew there was a real world somewhere, and that it wasn't here. Not in the *shtetl*, where the reek and noise and pervading whisper of cold wind through primeval branches, suffocated his most fervent prayers. The success of other artists became a daily torment to him. Laboring over drawings of unicorns and giant toadstools in his attic room above his squalid kitchen, he waited for the gallery owners to come calling. He listened for the sound of a patron's coach rattling along the cobblestones to take him away from this buried shithole at the edge of the *puszcza*. For a wealthy mistress to favor him, to hold a salon in his honor. But no one came.

In his dwindling spare time he continued to copy the old masters in the hope of self-improvement; he raced to meet deadlines for competitions and shows in the cities (the ones with no entry fee); he sent his work away by mail coach at no little expense, never to hear back. He began to lose his hair.

Just when things couldn't get worse, Ahava confronted him with the news that her sister had died in childbirth, leaving behind a baby girl and a much older husband already bent toward the grave. But when Yoske protested that he could barely put food on the table as it was, Ahava gently reminded him that she grew up in the poorhouse.

"God forbid," she said, "that I should consign my own flesh and blood to the same fate."

With any luck, the sickly child might not last the year—but Yoske had long put aside his faith in luck. He began to suffer headaches and joint pain. He fell behind in his work and his prayers. He wore a velvet cap like Rembrandt, a crown of failure. He knew there was talk in the marketplace of Ahava's threadbare skirts, and how she'd begun to bake cookies again to help make ends meet. His studio was stacked with unfinished consignments, copies of Rembrandts, Michalowskis—and other unspeakable images besides. But all he could do was spend more and more time at the tavern with the baker's boy, now grown into a tubby father of two, with dandruff and a large loose mouth. And so it was that at the tavern on a frosty late November evening, Lewi told Yoske about an old manuscript he'd come across in a storage shed at the back of his employer's house.

"It's the strangest thing you've ever seen," he said, wiping beer off his chin with his sleeve. "It was in an old trunk the boss asked me to toss, along with a cartload of other junk."

Written in an unknown language, it contained, Lewi said, strange diagrams and equations plus drawings of impossible creatures—eight-legged wolves, two-faced sorcerers, and wanton she-devils.

"But here's the kicker." Lewi leaned in and lowered his voice. "There's a map, see? Of the forest."

"A map?"

Everyone knew the forest was impenetrable.

"Not only a map," said the baker's boy, "but one with the directions for finding a craven hag in the forest rightly called a *mekhashefah*, because of her dealings with the Evil One."

Yoske felt prickles at the back of his neck. He begged Lewi to bring the book to him, offering some sketches from his "private" collection in exchange. The baker's boy readily agreed.

"Don't tell my wife," he winked, big man that he was.

All through the night Yoske pored over the illustrations and obscure scribbles—alone in his attic room, forgetting his supper, and barely noticing the infant Ariel's unrelenting squall—until finally the stars began to fade. Then, knowing it was now or never, he emptied his savings from a pickle jar and snuck downstairs as quietly as he could, but Ahava was waiting for him.

"At least take her a gift," his wife's weary voice came out of the shadows beside the unlit fire. "Some honey cake or a rabbit for her stew. *Mekhashefah* or not, it's rude to arrive with coins alone."

But Yoske was already gone.

Having memorized the map, he was deep within the forest before the moon had slipped below the treetops, a sticky mist rising to his ankles. The smell of primeval rot made it hard to breathe, the hush so thick he pulled his cap down over his head so he wouldn't have to listen to it. His dead brother swaggered out from behind a bare branch, a hole in his chest from a Cossack's saber. The ghost of his father walked towards him with his arms outstretched and the finial above the old bathhouse door impaled in his forehead. Tears trickled down the dead man's translucent cheeks but never fell. The strangeness of it all made Yoske's hair stand up, but he stumbled on.

Eventually he arrived at a hut dwarfed by a giant oak. The roots surged in waves like the tide of a great brown river around a piece of flotsam, and not for the first time in his life Yoske trembled at forces outside his understanding. The door was open. He took a tentative step over the threshold, only to behold the most hideous hag he had ever seen. She was sitting at a table, her hooked nose as pocked as cold *kasza*.

"What do you want?" Her clawed hands were covered in feathers and gore. There was a strangled chicken on her lap.

"I want to be famous." The five simple words had been so long repressed that just saying them made Yoske begin to cry. "I want to be the most celebrated artist in all of Poland. I want the perfection of my work to bring men and women to their knees. I want my cellar to be piled high with silver. I want a red coach drawn by black horses."

"But what," the witch asked delicately sipping from a broken cup, "is it that the housepainter Yoske *really* wants?"

And before he could stop it, the answer flew from his lips like a sick bird and unfurled diseased wings on the table between them.

"Immortality."

His soul had finally found a name for it.

"And how is what you *want* to be done?" the witch asked with a phlegmy sigh.

Yoske tried to keep his voice from shaking. "You shall give me the power to summon the Darkness, that I may gain its ancient wisdom."

She poked indifferently at the coins he'd thrown on the table. They lay among scattered saucers and cups and bones—a bison vertebra, an avian skull or two, some tiny human phalanges. Yoske shuddered. He regretted not bringing her a gift as his wife had suggested.

Unable to bring himself to look at the hag directly, due to her backward-facing knees and yolky drool, Yoske found himself gazing instead into a mirror hanging on a nail above the fire behind her. Coming from some rank corner and cutting through the stink of lonely cabbage dinners and piss, he smelled the familiar bite of pigment and freshly stretched canvas.

Nothing could go back to the way it was—he knew this. It was easy to blame the baby (not even his) for robbing him of his dream, as it had robbed Ahava of her sleep. But it wasn't that. It was the *shtetl.*

Only way out is in a coffin.

Unless?

"Name your price," he said.

"It's more than you can pay." Her mouth did not move as she said it.

A jolt of energy rippled under his skin. "Anything," he rasped. "I'm not afraid."

The sorceress licked greasy moonshine from her lips. Taking a finger bone from the table, she spat on the tip and wrote in drool across a piece of paper. Yoske could just make out four distinct clumps of mysterious ciphers, glistening in the light of the fire like the snot that poured from the nose of his infant niece.

"What is it?" he asked.

"They are words," the witch said. "You will need to memorize them."

Yoske didn't think he could—the mucousy writing had already

begun to fade—but when he squeezed his eyes shut, the four words were burned on his retina.

And then, she passed him the finger and told him to dip it into a small saucer on the table that contained diluted quicksilver. He was trembling so much that it was all he could do not to drop the gruesome bone, but he did as the witch said. On the table had appeared, as if from nowhere, the smallest canvas he had ever seen. It was layered thickly with paint, not yet dry. It looked a little like the tripe on display in the Christian butchers, and his gorge rose to touch it. The crone told him to paint the four words in tiny silver strokes across the canvas, and once done, to blend it carefully into the bilious mess.

"Why?" he asked.

"It is an incantation," she explained. "To make you immortal. Isn't that what you wanted?"

But Yoske no longer knew. A rat scampered across the stove, perched on the rim of the *kasza* pot. He just wanted to get away from the witch and the hut which seemed smaller now than it was when he'd entered. He'd lost all sense of time. When he finished painting the silver words from memory, his fingers were cramped and the witch was snoring, the first fires of daylight blazing in the blind slits of her eyes. Waking with a start, she told him to go home, and to repeat the process, copying and concealing the memorized spell onto his work from that day on. Yoske shuddered to think of desecrating his art in this way, like a trouble-maker scratching obscenities onto the bathhouse wall, or a sailor defiling his flesh with ink.

"Timing is everything," she said. "The paint should be not quite dry, just sticky enough to conceal the curse but not to erase it completely."

"I thought you said it was an incantation." He felt a jolt of fear shoot up his urethra, even as he knew it was too late for that.

She giggled like a street walker. "One man's prayers are another's curse." With a nauseating crack of her backwards-facing knees, she stood and passed the tiny canvas back to him. "You'll need this. It's all that's left of your soul."

Yoske did not stop running until he was at the edge of the forest, an egg swelling on his head where he collided with a low-hanging branch. Flakes of snow had begun to swirl before he crossed the threshold. Ahava was already stirring, but he went straight up to his garret and did as the crone said, painting and blending the unholy silver ciphers into an unfinished painting of an ogre and a gutsy princess. He began to regret it the moment he began, for the work was one of the best things he'd ever done—a rare inside cover engraving for a German publisher. A sin to vandalize in such a manner.

But just as he was about to bring a wet rag to the curse and wipe it from his painting forever, the earth shifted beneath the little house. The babe whimpered. The floor cracked open, but instead of the kitchen below with Ahava stirring the morning fire there was just a yawning darkness. He stepped back from the abyss, tripping over his own feet and falling to his knees. And so it was, from this position, that the artist-in-waiting first saw his answered prayers. Crawling over the lip of the crevice with an insectile nimbleness, was a demon whose waxen skin ran with pale ichor. Scarlet thorns squirmed like worms on its scalp. It extended a hand. Yoske smelled smoke. Thinking that the demon was offering to help him to his feet, he reached out a hand in return, but the demon shook its thorny head.

"I'll take that now," it said, gesturing toward the tiny canvas on which the remains of the artist's soul had dried to powdery clay. "If you don't mind."

And suddenly the artist didn't mind at all.

Yoske didn't flatter himself that it was the Evil One in the flesh. But an emissary was good enough, and this one seemed very efficient. It pulled a prepared agreement from an inside pocket, which Yoske signed in blood taken from a wound in his arm.

Things changed quickly after that.

Yoske's demon suggested that he offer to paint the Christian landowners. In portrait work, Yoske discovered a prowess that he always knew he had. His clients said that it was like looking into a mirror. In certain lights, the figures seemed to mimic more than the likenesses, but their movement as well, the very breath that quickened beneath the silks and velvets, pauldrons and jewels that Yoske so loved to paint—all the better to conceal the quicksilver curse.

The artist's fame spread. Critics struggled for words to describe the uncanny perfection of his work. He moved his family to Lublin and bought a great villa which he hung with a hundred mirrors to reflect in their eternal glittering the artist—not as he hoped to be, but as he finally was. He cut his hair and his beard and changed his name to Jòsef Zilberman in honor of the invocation which he carefully concealed in the gilt-framed portraits of burghers and heiresses. Jòsef Zilberman, son of a *shtetl* house painter, soon became the most celebrated artist in all Lublin, if not all of Poland.

One thing still bothered him, still niggled at the last vestiges of humanity he clung to, and that was his old friend, Lewi, the baker's boy. He wished to send for him to live with the great artist in his villa, to take him carousing in the dance halls and taverns. Over the months it became less and less amusing to do it alone. But the demon refused. He must leave all that behind, the slippery devil said. "You're in the real world now." And it rattled the contract that Jòsef, when he was Yoske, had signed in blood.

"Oh that," the artist said glumly.

The demon reminded him of the cellars stacked with silver, slower cousin to the chemical element that sped him to fame and fortune. It reminded him of the spacious studio taking up the whole upper story of the villa, with marble statues in a roof garden and views across the city of domes and spires. It reminded him of the red coach and black horses.

"You have everything you asked for," the demon said. "Everything you ever wanted."

But immortality came at a price. The artist now known as Zilberman worked for days on end with little sleep and no food, exhausted by the continual effort not to allow the demon's horned silhouette on the wall to overshadow his own. Only work kept the doubt and fear away. That and his nefarious drinking companions; mistresses who waited for him on silken sheets. But he was still human after all. He had been granted immortality at the cost of happiness. Of love, a word he torturously remembered but had forgotten how to say. He could no longer look Ahava in the eye, and the child would have nothing to do with him.

The work was everything, but it was never enough. He yearned to paint something else—the flowers growing in pots on the roof, the cat sleeping in the sun, to make art for its own sake. But the puling demon never left his side. A portrait was barely off to the framers, the secret invocation blended into the oily eyebrows of a wealthy merchant or the false smile of a courtesan, before his vermillion-haired "secretary" announced some esteemed English duke, Iberian caliph, or Italian general demanding that the artist's genius give them life after death. It was a cold comfort for the artist to learn that he was not alone in these eternal hungers that fed the demon souls in spades.

"You can't live on art alone," Ahava said one night, struggling out of her corset.

But somehow, he could. And somehow, he did.

2

The very lifelikeness of her husband's art chilled Ahava Zilberman to the bone. Less portraits than perfect doubles, she thought, his merchants and bishops looked like they could step out of their frames and into the world—and *would*, when no one was looking.

Ahava had seen horrors worse than this in the poorhouse, but in desperation, she summoned the rabbi to their hall of mirrors. He left after half an hour.

"There is nothing I can do for this man," the rabbi said. "Do not send for me again."

Ahava missed Yoske, the dreamer. She missed the softness in his eyes when she'd loosen her dark braids, back after they were first married. She wanted to go home, to walk again between the shaded tombstones of the mother and father she could barely remember and the twin sister she would never forget. Now her husband was lost to her, and the witch in the woods was to blame. But poverty was the worst kind of sorcery, and Ahava had no fear of witches. She decided to confront the meddling hag who had taken her life away.

After an exhausting five-day ride back on the mail coach, Ahava stepped through the door of her own house again. She left her niece, Ariel, in the care of Lewi's wife, and then ventured into the forest. New growth unfurled from the winter rot. Birdsong brightened her spirits; the sun was the color of fresh butter spreading between the nodding branches. Wolves sleepily skulked but let her pass. Arriving at her destination, Ahava looked up in wonder at the towering oak hung with vivid moss like a wizard's cloak in one of her husband's illustrations. The old sorceress stood at the door of the hut beside a young goat. She had a brush in her hands and smears of paint on her pocked nose.

"I've been expecting you," she said.

Ahava put the honey cake she'd remembered to bring with her upon the kitchen table. Scattered across it was an unfinished canvas draped in shadow, assorted jars and brushes. Ahava stepped boldly in and did not recoil at her host's pocked skin or backward-facing knees.

"I want to buy back the soul of my husband," Ahava began.

The witch shook her kerchiefed head. "It will cost more than you can pay," she said.

"Anything," Ahava said fiercely. "Tell your master—"

"I serve no master," the crone snapped.

Ahava apologized, but did not lower her eyes.

The witch leaned forward and sniffed Ahava's hair. Her frown softened. "Call me Tante, child." The goat gently butted Ahava's arm in agreement.

The witch explained that the artist formerly known as Yoske invoked his dark mastery by concealing an ancient curse in his paintings. "Four words, painted in quicksilver."

"In all of them?" Ahava asked in amazement. That explained their cursed lifelikeness. In the poorhouse, the old ones and foundlings had babbled about such things. Why had she not seen it before? Love, she thought. Love made me blind.

The witch nodded, and a tear trickled down her gruesome cheek.

"Is there no cure?" It was worse than Ahava thought. The shadows of the hut closed in. The witch's breath became labored, the hitched growl of an old dog.

"The cure is the sickness," she said.

Ahava blinked her eyes several times to make the room stop spinning. "I am afraid." she said.

"Well, that's a start." Dipping a brush into a saucer of quicksilver paint on the table, the witch took Ahava's trembling hand in her own clawed one, and guiding her thus, showed her how to inscribe and blend four strange words onto the canvas, which turned out to be a not-quite-dry painting of the pet goat, in a place just near its whiskery chin. Ahava's tongue felt unpleasantly thick. Her fingers cramped. She grew cold, and more nauseous than before.

The witch then explained how this was the curse her husband had bought in exchange for his soul and the souls of all he held dear. The room spun around Ahava, and she gripped the table. "Me?"

The witch nodded sadly. "He invoked the calling of art upon you too, and all who come after," she said. "The only hope is to transform the curse into a blessing."

"Transform?" Ahava said. "Not undo?"

"There is no undoing the curse of art," the witch cautioned. "There is only living with it, for better or worse."

What choice did Ahava have?

The witch leaned in close, so close that Ahava could smell the vodka on her breath and the honey cake besides. With ulcerated lips the crone whispered into Ahava's ear a fifth word. The word was meaningless, but its syllables buzzed inside her head, like a bee trapped behind a window. And then the crone ground mercury and melted sulfur in a saucer, with a little bit of vodka from a paint-smeared glass. At first the paste turned a tarry black, blacker even than the unlit hut. But now, it transformed into a dazzling vermillion that generated its own light, like dragon breath from a fairy tale. The smell gave Ahava an instant headache, like the flatulence of a thousand goats, and the red was so pure that it hurt. Like sacrifice. The ache of love.

Next, the witch made Ahava dip a fine brush in the vermillion paint. She guided her hand in the painting of the fifth word after the silver ones, but just near the goat's pink tongue, and instructed Ahava to blend it carefully, concealing it but not erasing it completely. It was difficult, precise work, but in the process, Ahava felt her chest unclench, the shadows in the hut recede.

"The fifth word," the witch explained, gulping thirstily from the filthy glass, "is what changes the meaning of the sentence, transforming the curse of darkness into the blessing of light."

"What does it mean?"

"You will know in time." The crone licked vodka off her chin with a long black tongue. "If that is what you want."

Sitting in the dark hut with the pungent smell of goat and paint and the *kasza* popping and spitting in its cauldron, Ahava recalled how Yoske had taken her in, saving her and later her little niece from the poorhouse when no one else would.

"I do," she said, because she would always love him.

"Memorize the words," the witch said.

But Ahava already had.

"Never forget," the witch said.

And Ahava never would.

"Conceal the vermillion word, the fifth, into one of your husband's unfinished paintings directly after the quicksilver curse already inscribed. Ensure the paint is still sticky to the touch or the blessing will not take. Do you understand, my child?"

Ahava nodded. "Yes, Tante."

The witch then mixed a pot of the vermillion pigment for Ahava to take with her, warning her not to breathe the fumes in too deeply or too often.

"It's bad for the baby," the witch said.

Ahava put her hand to her belly, to the quickening of new life inside her.

"Not to mention it might drive you mad," the witch said, through a suppurated mouthful of honey cake. "Mercury, you know."

"I did not know that, Tante," Ahava said politely, "not being an artist myself."

"You are one now," the old one muttered.

Ahava thanked her and then she hurried home, stopping to pat the goat on her way out.

━✦╿╲╾

Back in Lublin, the church bells rang the midnight hour. Inside the villa, Ahava recoiled from the reflections of a hundred broken mirrors. The shadow of her torch flailed as she ran up interminable flights of stairs. Finally, reaching the roof, she hesitated at the threshold of her husband's studio. She had never set foot in it, not just because of his clear instructions (laced with an unspoken warning) but also because she had never wanted to. Until now. Now something drew her forward, despite the sweat trickling down the small of her back. It wasn't just knowing what she had to do. It was a sudden desire to do it, that had overcome whatever loathing had stopped her until now. Whatever lay behind that door, she wanted to see it. The dampness above her buttocks was not just that of fear. It was also that of desire.

Outside the windows of the penthouse, trees from the ornamental garden stood as still as sculptures, washed silver in the moonlight. Ahava's fingers sought the spare key, and found it tucked in a slot concealed above the door frame. She opened the door, and gasped. Her feet teetered at the edge of a crack in the floor, and the hairs at the back of her neck rose as she watched it cut a widening swathe across the tiles, flinging them up in fragments at its edge. She clung to the door frame to avoid falling in. Taking a deep breath and sending a prayer, more felt than spoken, to a God who had lately forsaken her, she leapt across the fissure while she could, falling to her knees on the opposite side. Then, she half crawled, half stumbled around stacked canvases and stretchers, a table strewn with pallets and jars of murky water, until she stopped, panting, beside a walnut desk piled with letters of commission that reached almost to the ceiling. Now, illuminated by the moon falling through a skylight, the white bones of Yoskc's easel came into view. A canvas gleamed wetly, its edges shrouded in gloom so that the image upon it flickered in the light of Ahava's torch, like a dream. The painting, in oil, depicted a high tower in a monolithic stone castle. Ahava's heart thundered; she reached a hand to the image, brought it back to her chest. In the tower was a turret window in which stood a richly dressed person of indeterminate sex. It was painted with a metallic cord wound about the neck and trussing the face—a tongue lolled between lips open in a scream. It was perfectly lifelike, and in this very quality, horrifyingly *lifeless*. Especially when it, unmistakably, moved.

The figure struggled to breathe, struggled to be free.

Ahava backed away in disbelief and horror, until she felt a table behind her, blocking her escape. She sobbed and felt the hot spill of tears. The taste of salt. Forcing herself to bring a trembling finger to the paint, she ascertained that it was still sticky to the touch. Then, she took up a magnifying glass from the table to confirm that her husband had concealed the witch's curse in the silver cord. The tiny silver scrawled swam beneath the glass. Nausea returned and she swallowed it down. Her nape tingled at the heat rising from the hole in the floor behind her, an unwelcome presence that darkened the edges of her vision. She blinked and it was gone. Using the torch to light a candle on the desk, she took up a brush as fine as a single eyelash. She poured some of Tante's vermillion paint onto the palette. The red glowed and pulsed as it did in Tante's hut, like a beating heart. That seemed to turn some gear behind her ribs, some mechanism engaged within her, and the fear ebbed. She was able to work quickly then, dipping the brush in the red paint to inscribe the fifth word and then blend it onto the canvas, somewhere near the raw red throat of the screaming mouth.

Immediately it was done, the painted garotte fell away from the painted face. The hideous crack along the stone floor shrieked slowly closed, broken fragments of tiles reassembling themselves. Stars began to wheel across the dome of the sky painted across her husband's canvas, bathing Ahava in wondrous light. Her eyes rolled back in her head and unconsciousness hit like a tidal wave, washing her thoughts into a house of ill repute—where a doxy forced a blade into the heart of the artist Zilberman, who uttered a low cry, fell to his knees, and was soon dead.

The last word on his lips was the name of his beloved wife, the orphan girl Ahava.

Over the next days she burned all her husband's paintings that she could get her hands on, offering to buy them back from galleries and collectors at inflated prices. She smashed all the mirrors lest any reflection remain of the artist's corroded heart. Then she travelled home to the village and collected Ariel from the neighbor. The woman's husband—the new baker Lewi—wept at the news of Yoske's death and promised he'd say Kaddish for his old friend.

In time Ahava gave birth to a daughter. Penniless after settling her husband's debts, and with three mouths to feed, she didn't know what to do.

"Why not take up his profession?" Tante asked with a sly shrug.

Ahava thought about it. After all, there were other widows—the butchers and the millers—who had done the same. Why not her?

"Better than the poorhouse," the witch said without moving her lips, and not for the first time, Ahava was more than a little afraid of her.

"Don't forget to conceal the curse and also the blessing in every painting," Tante said.

"Whatever for?" Ahava asked. "Yoske's dead."

"The curse of art does not die with the artist's flesh," the witch mumbled without quite meeting Ahava's eye, "nor its blessing either."

"I want nothing to do with it," Ahava said, and went back to baking cookies for the marketplace.

But it was hard to bake with a newborn and a colicky niece. And flour and sugar didn't grow on trees, never mind wood for the fire. But it was more than that. She felt drawn to her husband's old studio, and often found herself looking up at the ceiling as if to see through to the blank canvases stacked therein, just waiting for the artist's touch. In the end, what choice did she have? She began by completing her husband's book illustrations. It was hard at first, but she found herself bounding up the steps to the attic studio at every chance she had, eager to take up where household duties had made her leave off. Every outlined genie or elf or pirate king she colored and shaded made her ache for poor Yoske. But even as she artfully improved upon him, not only in the blending of the four silver words behind a gossamer wing or unicorn horn, the fifth in red toadstool, but also in the honing of her unique talent, she rose to the competition with herself, to be better than she was. She paid off her debts, could afford medicine for Ariel. The booksellers agreed she exceeded her husband's talent and they begged for more.

But in art and in life, Ahava belonged to the real world, and it wasn't long before Ahava Zilberman had earned a name for herself as a *shtetl* artist. Collectors and buyers came from Vienna and Warsaw—even as far away as New York, in America. There was not a buyer or critic who didn't rave about how in the limpid imperfection of the widow's work lay the beginning of all hope.

It was hard going. The hours were long. The cost was high, and sometimes, when the baby cried, or the housework mounted up or when Ahava's joints swelled and burned, her thoughts and love flew to Yoske and how he'd labored alone over an art that never loved him back. Participating in a competition with himself that he could never win. She knew that she had inherited the curse he'd summoned, but she forgave him, even loved him more for it. Art was after all a madness. She could feel it worming around her own heart sometimes too, and only counting the baby's toes or a visit to her sister's grave would pull her back from the abyss. One day she came across her husband's tattered old sketchbook in the back of a drawer. She thought of burning it, but instead kept it as a reminder of how the distinction between dream and dreamer is not always easy to find.

Ahava never remarried.

In time, Tante said, there would be no need of the soul-sapping ritual, the attention and effort it took to transform the curse into the blessing of art, so that all would feel its light and love. But when? When would it end? How much time? How much red paint,

Ahava wondered, would it take before the door her husband opened was finally closed, and the Evil One shut out forever?

"May as well ask, How long is a piece of string?" was the only answer she got, which was no answer at all.

Time and tears. Ahava painted the blessing onto her art and into the world and even into one or two permanent exhibitions in the city. The fawning collectors and critics urged her to move, but Ahava was happy in the *shtetl*. She belonged here, to these people, to her children, and above all to the protective shade of the *puszcza* into which she ventured every Sunday with a basket of wine and honey cakes under her arm. Alone but for her mangy, half-blind goat, the old woman welcomed the company, for she already loved Ahava as her own.

Love made Ahava an artist.

Maybe it was for that reason that the artist-widow begged of her "fairy godmother" one more favor—that her own daughter be spared the cursed blessing of artistic talent, and every daughter in their line from that time on.

"Are you sure?" Tante asked. No need to remind Ahava that anything can be had at a price.

"I am," said Ahava.

Which is how it came to be that it was not Ahava's *daughter,* but her beloved niece, the child Ariel, who inherited the artist's curse. Soon adept with brush and pigment, the needful child was never so happy (some would say) as with a palette in one hand and a brush in the other. Her tongue poking out the side of her mouth, she learned how to blend the quicksilver curse, quickly followed by the vermillion blessing, into first her aunt's work and then her own: the innkeeper's apron, the grey eyes of a humble gravedigger, or the pearly gleam of a *mezuzah* after the rain.

HOMESICK

Alex finishes *Homesick #30* in her upper-floor studio at Cinnabar Collective on the last day of March. It is her thirtieth birthday and the one-year anniversary of Aunt Abby's death—a time to remember, a time of bright autumnal mornings and the trill of bats at night. The work is part of a series of houses, apartments, beach shacks, trailers—each numbered and tinged with the artist's signature silvery light.

Alex is a rising name in the art world at last. People call her a wunderkind, a genius. Abby would blow a raspberry if she were alive. *Infernal prowess transformed through human imperfection into art,* like that explained it.

Twelve months ago, when Alex joined the collective, she was just one of the resident artists. But, after only a year, what everyone knows about her now is that she is about to be famous. Critics use words like "bewitching" and "necessary" for her paintings. Art magazines describe her work as "replete with joyful play" despite the "argent hues and unsettling imagery that spills over the edges of the frame like liquid light".

Alex's light-filled studio space is on the top floor of the reclaimed warehouse. Her easel stands in a Star Trek-like beam of sun from the lofty skylights. She dips a miniature Kolinsky sable brush into cadmium red for the finishing touches to *Homesick #30.* But then she pauses to remember, on this day of all days, that they'd once used vermillion. A word, her aunt had told her, derived through Old French *vermeillon* from the Latin *vermiculus,* or "little worm", after the tiny, scaled bugs from which the dye was originally obtained.

Shit, Alex thinks. *I'm actually crying.*

The painting is of a beach house in a remote bay on the NSW South Coast, leaden eaves stark against a pond-green sky. A figure stands in the attic window overlooking the unseen ocean. Using silver paint, Alex has ritualistically blended the first four words of the ancient invocation into an unsettling glimmer about the eyes. The paint is not diluted quicksilver like her ancestors used (*stuff will drive you mad if you let it,* Abby said), yet the clusters of symbols still make her shudder—a nasty complexity to them that eludes easy duplication and changes according to one's perspective, or mood, or the light. The real art is in blending them just to the brink of erasure. One would have to use a magnifying glass to see, and even then.

Alex reaches with the vermillion tip of the brush, but doesn't quite touch the figure's mouth when there's a voice behind her.

"That red is next-level."

She freezes with the brush not quite at the canvas. She slowly turns at the unwelcome interruption. It's a designer called Winter, who bears a frosted cupcake on a plate.

"Amazing." Winter hangs back in the doorway, staring wide-eyed at the painting. "It's beautiful, Alex."

Alex's creative mind finds words like "beautiful" and "amazing" a little lazy. She fears being interrupted in her work, especially at this point with the paint drying and the family curse not yet transformed into a blessing. Some of the light seems to have left the space around the canvas. Her aunt was very clear about the importance of the fifth word.

Of course, Winter doesn't know about this part of Alex's process, passed down from a long line of Polish artists—all women, mostly aunts. No one does.

Winter holds out the cupcake, and when Alex doesn't come forward, she steps through the doorway and gingerly places it on a bench crammed with jars, dead paint tubes and books. Despite adoring Alex, Winter is the most self-contained person she has ever met. Her aura of a concentrated, defiant stillness makes Alex see her friend in heightened color: the Monet lavender of her eyes, the warm russet of her hair, starry dust motes floating along the dun slats of the old floorboards for which Alex feels a wrench of nostalgia as if for something lost, or about to be.

"Happy birthday, babe," Winter says quietly.

Alex says, "Are you growing out your fringe?"

Winter swipes her hair away from her eyes, and then points to the painting. "Haunted house. I love it."

Alex pivots back to the painting. She doesn't pay the critics, or anyone, much attention, but "haunted"? That word bothers her even more than "amazing" and "beautiful", and when she turns back to Winter, her smile feels too wide for her face. "What makes you think it's haunted?"

Until she was thirteen and her mother put a stop to it, Alex had spent every Sunday at Aunt Abby's studio. She'd learned about art, but also *their* art—that of blending four words in silver, the color of thought, of creation, before adding a fifth in vermillion, the color of the heart and of love, into every painting. Her aunt's subjects were mostly cats with flowers, the ancient conjure concealed in the glister of a tabby's eye, the flapping tongue of a hibiscus. The fifth word was critical. Necessary, you could say. Abby had traced the origins of the process way back to the diabolical dealings of a nineteenth-century Polish artist who'd brought the curse of art down on his family, although her aunt was always a little fuzzy on the specifics. "Jòsef Zilberman was your great-great-great-great-great-something uncle . . . others say that we aren't related at all . . . it's just rumors and guesses . . . there's a sketchbook somewhere . . . who knows what really happened?"

What they do know is that all five words are needed for the curse to be transformed into a blessing.

Winter steps up to link her arm playfully in Alex's. "That person there in the window. Is she trying to get in or out?"

Alex knows a haunted house when she sees one, but the blessing is supposed to protect her work from any lingering bad intent—as Aunt Abby warned, the soul you save might be your own. But now the pulse of light around the house *has* taken on an ominous note, and yes, there *is* something snaking around the figure in the window, twisting it gruesomely, the limbs unnaturally foreshortened. And that spindly leg—did she mean to paint it backwards? Pure terror emergent in that quicksilver gaze.

The blessing has yet to be written.

"Shit!" Alex quickly unlinks her arm from Winter's. Positioning her body between her friend and the easel, she touches the paint with her finger and is dismayed to find it just past the point of stickiness—the point of letting go. Should she destroy the damn thing? But it's a masterpiece, one of her best yet. It might even sell for enough to bring Alex closer to her dream of getting her own studio down the coast, far away from confusing distractions like Winter. So, with the red paint, she quickly adds the fifth word across the figure's mouth. It's less a word than a thought-form, and the weird ciphers still make her feel a little like throwing up—and not just because of the horror of vandalizing one of her own paintings in this way.

When she stands back, she is relieved to see that *Homesick #30* has reverted to what she'd conceived it to be: a weather-beaten holiday house nestled in a sheltered bay, the kind of place an artist might go to retreat from the world. The figure in the dormer window has almost straightened up, an unplanned kink to their posture, sure, but their folded arms have assumed the correct proportions, and their legs are turned the right way around as if to return to unfinished work.

"There!" Alex says. "Nothing haunted about it."

But Winter's mood, always unpredictable, has shifted. Maybe hurt by Alex's irritability, or that she didn't thank Winter for the cupcake, she scrolls through her messages, glossed lips parted in a not-quite smile. Alex loves Winter, just not in *that* way, and besides, Alex has a boyfriend, Kaleb-with-a-K as her mother calls him, braying, *"I should warn you, Kaleb-with-a-K, that my daughter is incapable of loving anything but her work."* And while that happens to suit an up-and-coming musician just fine, it wouldn't suit Winter. At all.

Winter wants a baby.

She turns away, engrossed in one of her dating or adoption apps.

Abby once told Alex about some *shtetl* widow back in Poland who tried to protect her daughter from the wicked witch of art and sacrificed an orphaned niece instead. From that point on, the story goes, artistic genius skipped the mothers in their family, and instead has been passed down through aunts, guardians, godmothers, second cousins—just not actual mothers.

"Ariel Zilberman adored her aunt, apparently. Shadowed her like a cat. Took to her room when the old lady died and never came out. Which just goes to show," Abby had said, accidentally sloshing vodka into Alex's lemon cordial, *"mothers are good for some things. Just not everything."*

Later, when she thinks about why she does what she does next, Alex has no way of explaining it. Winter has stepped out of the space and is about to turn down the narrow hallway when Alex quickly signs the painting, using a pencil lying around, and calls out to her friend.

"Winter, wait!" She takes *Homesick #30* off the easel and goes into the zig-zag passageway where Winter has wandered off toward the staircase. "You can have it."

Winter keeps walking. Flips Alex a middle finger, still bent over her phone.

"No, I mean it." Alex steps forward and Winter turns around. "I want you to take the painting."

"What the absolute fuck?" Winter's milky brow furrows in suspicion.

"A birthday gift," Alex says holding the painting out to her friend. "Who says you can't give as well as receive gifts on your birthday?"

"I can't take it, Alex."

"It might be worth a fortune someday."

Aunt Abby never gave away a painting in her life. Free art being a contradiction in terms, she always said.

"Please," Alex says, because Abby is dead, and life is like a dream. Is she actually floating? A slice of time slips away, and Winter is suddenly holding the painting out before her the way one might hold a crying baby out by its armpits. A play of shadow makes the canvas convulse in her grasp.

"It's okay," Alex says. "It won't bite."

Winter's lavender eyes darken in disbelief. "I don't want it."

"You don't like it? I thought—"

"No. I mean yes. I love it. I think. But my place is tiny. I don't have the wall space."

"I'll come over on the weekend and help you find some." Alex knows it's unfair to be alone with Winter, and might send the wrong message, but suddenly Alex isn't sure of what message she wants to send—if maybe it's changed. "We'll figure it out."

Winter holds the painting out between them and her arms tremble with the effort, as though the painting is struggling against her. "What if you need it back one day?"

"Like if I end up a broken failure?" Alex gently folds her friend's arms around the canvas so that it nestles against her chest. "All the more reason for you to take care of it for me."

‸⫶⫶‸

Alex never met her father, an American soldier on furlough for one night in Sydney before going back to get himself blown up in Afghanistan. Alex's mother later married, giving birth to two boys in her forties, her new family taking up all her time. It fell to Alex, now at art school, to take care of her aunt, the great artist Abigail Silber brought low by illness and intemperance, bent half-double, her arthritic knees swollen and twisted.

Once at the pub, listening to Winter describe a long-ago family holiday with cousins and canoes, it occurred to Alex that she had no happy memories from her early childhood. Just weirdness and tension. Her only real connections with any kind of reality were her weekends with Aunt Abby in a beach shack long buried under a fancy new development. It was there, surrounded by secret relations of time and place, of light and dark, that she felt safe. That she felt loved.

Art made her safe. Art gave her love.

In Abby's final days, Alex had desperately graffitied the secret invocation in every hidden corner of the place—wherever shadows slouched, in the cracks of doorways and the fissures of unsettled beams: streaks of sticky silver and glops of red slithering at the edge of the eye. The ugly ciphers looked like tags from hell, and no solvent could ever remove them completely. Their shadow lingered long after the house was repainted for sale. All for nothing. Because Alex had been unable to save her aunt. Back then, she simply wasn't a good enough artist.

As Winter disappears down the hall, juggling the painting, something falls to the floor from her pocket. It's a business card. Alex bends down to pick it up, batting away the eye-floaters—*muscae volitantes*, Latin for "flying flies"—which plague her when she's been working too hard. The card is for some photographer called Emma Ford. Maybe one of the new residents? A slow heat creeps up Alex's ribs and throat. For a moment, she struggles for breath, futilely chasing the shadows of vitreous debris across her retina with her shifting gaze. The card begins to reshape itself into a fat worm twisted around her fingers. In an ugly reflex, she flicks it away, watching it crawl after her friend in a flash of uncertain light.

➤ノ｜ヽ◀

The next day a gallery sells six of Alex's paintings to a Hong Kong buyer for an unprecedented amount, so she decides to take Friday night off and celebrate her birthday at the pub instead of alone with her brushes and Winter's cupcake. She posts an invitation for drinks on the studio's social page. "First and last rounds are on me!" she writes.

Winter has not been back at work since Alex gifted her the painting. Surprisingly, Alex misses the random intrusions.

She wanders through the labyrinthine old warehouse, ending up downstairs in Winter's space with all the other designers. The windowless cubicles bristle with monitors and keep cups, the designers at their desks wrapped in headphones.

Winter's cubicle remains empty.

She thinks about having given away the painting, and wonders if it was too much. Or not enough.

Late on Friday night at the pub, Alex has drunk herself almost sober. She's bought more rounds than she should, masking her disappointment that Winter hasn't shown behind a largesse she doesn't feel. Even Kaleb has taken time off from rehearsals to join the small group of needful creatives who have come for the free booze and the chance that some of Alex's good fortune will rub off on them.

There is a painful lump in Alex's throat. The pub overlooks the train tracks to the west and Princess Highway to the south. It is two hundred years old, an old haunt of factory workers, metal die-casters, leather tanners, hatmakers. Its stark façade and easy egress across the train tracks makes it a magnet for graffiti artists, billposters, and rope-climbing poop painters. No sooner has the previous night's vandalism been washed off or painted over than new tags, obscenities, messages and masterpieces appear. The south wall especially is so thickly encrusted that it looks three-dimensional. Inside, it smells like onions and cologne and beer. Over against the wall a large spittoon overflows with brown mucous. *Impossible.* Alex blinks and the spittoon is once more a receptacle for nothing but lint and scrunched napkins from the bistro. Mercury from the hat factories could still be in the air. How else to explain the kink in her perception? Drunken customers dare each other to stand in the infamous "cold spot" near the bar where a hat worker hanged herself from an exposed beam. Alex knows—in a part of herself that will deeply regret the fourth or fifth vodka martini—that art *can* bend life, generating illusions that make you want to hurt or be hurt. Is that its curse?

Her therapist said the grief would take two years to lift, maybe more. But Alex doesn't want it to lift. It's all she has left of her aunt.

Just then, Winter bursts in, clutching the arm of a breath-taking woman. Amazing. Beautiful. She is taller than Winter, and a little older, with a crest of titanium hair and a preternaturally long and elegant neck, like a swan.

"This is Emma," Winter says, blushing. "She's a photographer."

Alex remembers the card that fell out of her friend's pocket. When Kaleb, instantly smitten, asks Emma what her subjects are, she intones, "Brats and brides," like it's something she's said a hundred times before.

Alex's birthday is soon forgotten. Kaleb insists on one for the road, cheerfully putting another round of $20 cocktails on Alex's tab. The drinks arrive and Kaleb dares Emma to stand in the mad hatter's cold spot, and she does, stepping out quickly with an alarmed "ugh!". Winter's skin is dewy. Her DIY fringe hangs in damp tendrils over her eyes, which have darkened to indigo in the gloom of the pub. Her beer bottle is smeared with lip gloss, and there is a butterfly-shaped hickey on her throat. Alex gropes her way to the bathroom and throws up in the toilet bowl. She's rinsing her mouth at the sink when the door swings open and Emma bursts through in a gust of smoky perfume. She goes into a stall, and leaving the door ajar, sits on the toilet and lights up a joint. Alex averts her gaze to the ceiling, but there is only a fly-specked circle in the paint where the smoke alarm once was.

"So nice to finally meet the great Aleksandra Silber," Emma says. "The painting you gave Winter is haunting. Every time I look at it, I see something different."

A drop of sweat worms its way between Alex's shoulder blades. "Haunting?"

"The woman in the window trying to escape," Emma says. "Is that you?"

Alex feels a headache twinge—these questions are the kind her mother asks, and a true artist is entitled to her secrets. But this time it's different—what if the blessing didn't stick? What if the paint was too dry?

"Escape . . . " Alex echoes with a cough, stalling for time.

"Or die trying, huh?"

"How did you two meet?" Alex manages to ask.

"Funny story." Emma flushes the joint down the toilet and moves to the sink in two graceful strides. "It was the day you gave Winter *Homesick Number Thirteen*—"

"Thirty," Alex interrupts. "*Homesick Number Thirty*."

"—we had just finished a concept meeting with a mutual client. We all exchanged cards, and I had another meeting I had to race off to. I got lost in that infernal maze—went up instead of down, around instead of out, and finally I came across Winter . . . and . . . " Emma's hard, lovely face slackens, and Alex sees a pushing-forty burnout, once a promising ballerina who measured herself by the success of other dancers and came up wanting every time. Every lesson, each humiliating recital, her father's wasted money yapping at her heels. "She looked different than in the meeting. Totally gorgeous of course—those Edenic eyes—but more significant, somehow. She had your painting . . . "

Must get it back.

Emma stops to apply lipstick. "Buy you a drink? It's the least I can do."

"Thanks," Alex says. "Big day tomorrow."

Emma fluffs her pearlescent hair. "No rest for the wicked, huh?"

—⟋⟍—

Alex really does have a big day—she's already behind for the Homesick show scheduled for July. Over the following week, and halfway into the next, she tries to focus on finishing the rest of the series, remembering to repeat the ritual on every canvas. Their ancestors had used actual quicksilver for the first four words of the curse, invoked as a kind of atonement, Alex wondered, but Abby was never clear on that. The fifth word was more like a prayer—for forgiveness, maybe—and the vermillion had been ground from mercury sulfide. Over the generations, Abby said, the artists had replaced this with safer synthetic pigments. The only mixing Alex ever saw Abby do was for her medicinal highballs.

But Alex is distracted by Winter's absence, and her sunny space is soon cluttered with unfinished work—stranded houseboats that look more like ships in the night, tents slumped as caves, rust-eaten trailer-homes. She has texted Winter several times, reminding her about hanging the painting. Alex tries to think of some excuse to get it back—surely Winter will be nothing if not relieved.

But Emma—Alex can't help but think how Emma is all kinds of wrong. That neck, maybe. Those teeth, imperfectly imprinted on Winter's flesh. Later in the week, after a post-Netflix quickie, Alex asks Kaleb whether he feels Emma's wrongness too. He looks at her pityingly and turns around to go to sleep. So she doesn't ask him again. Instead, she dreams of Emma's disembodied teeth leaving marks all over her own skin.

Finally, Winter replies to her texts with a curt, *Sorry. Busy helping Emma get ready for a new show.*

Winter has always helped Alex with *her* shows—doing the media, stretching canvases, screening calls from her mother or Kaleb, ordering flowers. She's braided Alex's hair, organized the catering, mixed the playlist, worked the room . . . if Alex is honest, she couldn't have become Aleksandra Silber, the artist, without Winter.

Alex texts: *Have a better painting. Smaller for your tiny house. Can come over and hang it now.*

She adds a wine glass emoji.

After a long pause, almost an hour, Winter's text with a heart emoji comes through: *All good. Haunted painting hung! Love it.*

Alex stares at the screen for several minutes, and all that time her own heart seems not to beat.

Think. *Thing is,* Alex texts, *I need to borrow it back.*

She watches ellipses slide into silence. Then nothing. Another hour or two passes. *The painting?* And then, *Why?*

Homesick #30 was contracted for the brochure, social media etc. to get the buzz going. Lies and more lies. *Gallery insisting.*

That painting? Emma loves it too. WTF Alex?

#30 yeah

Alex watches the numbing march of ellipses.

Why did you give it to me then?

Sorry! Single tear emoji.

Because she really is.

"One-two-buckle-my-shoe," Aunt Abby said once when Alex asked her what the secret script was. "Pre-Sephardic gobbledygook from some Medieval kabbalist's grimoire or Persian mystic's parchment. Who knows?" She tipped another slug of hooch into her paint-smeared glass. "You know how those old alchemists loved their ciphers and cryptic symbolism."

Alex didn't. "And the fifth word? It looks different from the others. I mean aside from the color."

"Trust me," her aunt had said, before passing out in her chair. "You don't want to know."

But Alex did. She wanted it more than anything.

Finally, after several hours, the phone rings. It's Winter, talking in a hushed voice. There's a problem with returning the painting, she says. She's coming by Cinnabar tomorrow, a Saturday, to pick up some things. She'll explain then.

Alex sleeps in her studio that night, on a camp bed she has set up in a corner. Sheet metal on the roof lifts in the wind and she hears rats scuttle. Her dead soldier father comes to visit her, just a boy, half his chest torn off by shrapnel. Abby trots out of the easel with the legs of a goat and broken wings of a butterfly, a contradiction in terms. Alex barely closes her eyes after that. At dawn she goes downstairs to wait alone for Winter. The other designers are seldom there on the weekend. Winter turns up just after five. Alex is asleep on the floor.

"I only have a minute," Winter says, throwing things haphazardly into a duffle bag. "The car is double parked. I'm driving down to the property to join Emma."

Every bone in Alex's body hurts. She pushes herself to her feet. She feels a yawning hollow in her chest. Winter is nervous, and her vivid eyes dart and swoop like tropical fish. There are bruises around her wrists and hickeys at her collar bone, making her look more ethereal than ever.

"Emma's father was a painter. He converted an old church."

Alex licks her lips. It's an effort to speak, and her own voice sounds foreign to her. "Why would a wedding photographer need a show?"

"Jealousy's a curse." Winter clutches a keyboard in one hand and a dog-eared notebook in another.

"A curse?"

"You think you can throw some old painting at me, and I'll hang around forever?" Winter is on the verge of hysteria, two red flushes on her cheeks, tendrils of russet hair sticking messily to her face.

Your art is all that's left of your soul, Abby had said. *Never give it away for free.*

Is that the truth of it? If most of an artist's humanity is in their art, what of them is left for the real world? Or is that the wrong question? Alex never feels fully present outside her studio, where the real world reflects back from canvases, sketches—more truthful than in any mirror, or in the eyes of a lover, or mother. Or friend.

"Winter," she pleads. "Look at me. Here I am."

"Alex," Winter says gently, shaking her unbrushed hair from her face. "Emma and I are going to have a baby."

"What?"

Winter grabs a stylus and a candle and chucks them in her bag. "Our luck changed. Right after you gave us the painting—"

"I didn't give it to *her*, Winter," Alex says, not trying to hide the sourness in her voice. "I gave it to you."

But it's all messed up now—who she meant the painting for and what it wanted instead, and why.

"Right after you gave us . . . me . . . the painting, like the next day, Emma gets a call from Pidgeon Lane Projects inviting her to be a part of this big photography show there. One of the artists had to drop out because of a car accident—a terrible coincidence—so they needed a replacement. It's a miracle, like the painting was her lucky charm, she says. Or I was. She's not letting either of us go. Sorry."

A baby? A jolt of adrenaline shoots up from Alex's belly. "Listen, Winter, that painting—there's something wrong with it. I should have told you."

"No." Winter takes Alex's calloused, paint-crusted fingers in her own smooth ones. "It's perfect. A way for me to remember your birthday."

Alex doesn't answer because Winter steps out into the hall to take a call, and her face when she comes back into the studio is flushed like she's running a fever, like she's sick.

LOVESICK

Alex begins to stalk Emma Ford. At first it seems that she's a nobody—just some two-bit studio photographer who has recently started posting about her luck turning. "Just when I'd lost all faith in luck, haha," she quips online. Alex matches the date of the first Instagram post to a week after Alex gave the painting to Winter. Alex follows a link to an upcoming show for emerging photographers at Pidgeon Street Projects in spring, but the details are fuzzy. She is interrupted by a frantic email from her own gallery manager about trouble with the Hong Kong collector who wants to renege on part of his order. Over the next few days, the top floor of Cinnabar is inundated by rats.

Alex wakes up alone one night—Kaleb is on tour—to three missed calls from Winter, all made between two and 4am. She calls back, almost dropping the phone in her hurry, but her friend doesn't answer. She gets up and goes to the kitchen, trying Messenger, WhatsApp, FaceTime, and the rest, but Winter doesn't pick up. Standing at her breakfast bar, drinking vodka straight from the bottle, Alex finds Emma Ford's contact details from her website—but the call goes straight to voicemail.

She has no idea where Emma's property is or where to start looking. Instead of going back to bed, she takes the vodka and drives to the studio. The stars are just visible through the long, grimy skylights. Alex makes coffee. She turns on the Ikea lamp. She finishes a painting. It's of an Airstream trailer in the center of a paddock, with someone sitting at a dusty window watching the stars come out, and she carefully blends the fifth word in vermillion onto a glass of red wine just as the figure brings it to their lips.

Aunt Abby, sloshing another slug of Belvedere into a teacup, was always clear on two things. The first was that Not-Great-Uncle Zilberman—the name morphing over the generations into the diasporic "Silber"—was a piece of work, and the women in the family were still cleaning up his cursed mess. And the second was that there was no point in asking what the fifth word was. May as well just ask, How long is a piece of string?

Kaleb calls later that week after a gig and breaks up with her. They both cry. She curls up on the floor of her studio and closes her eyes. The infolding light of Kaleb's love compresses and fades, and in its place is an Airstream in the middle of a paddock beneath a spangled sky. Winter is standing naked at the window, a faint outline of wings on her swollen belly.

A call from her mother wakes Alex the next morning. She has moved to the camp bed, but she doesn't remember doing so. She is freezing, and her back throbs like it's been kicked in a bar brawl. Her mother says she ran across some of Alex's paintings at a show. "They're arresting. I give you that, if a little unwholesome. Abby always said that when it came to art, I should keep my mouth shut."

Alex is too tired to fight with her mother. She presses a hand into her lower back, eyeing the overturned bottle of vodka on the floor.

"Are you coming to the boys' birthday party next month?"

And maybe because her mother did not compliment her on her art, or mention Aunt Abby, or maybe it's because Alex doesn't know what kind of a daughter her mother wants her to be, she says she'll probably be too busy with her show.

"I'll send them something, promise."

"Not a painting, please just promise me that." Strained laughter. "Seriously, the brochure described you as an alchemist. I don't get it. Isn't that someone who turns lead into gold?"

Alex closes burning eyelids. "Actually, mother, alchemy is just any process of mysterious transmutation. Like form into feeling, or darkness into light."

"Or the reverse, I suppose, would equally apply?"

Before Alex can bite, a text comes in from Winter. *Miscarried.* Crying emoji.

━◢▮◣━

Alex's Homesick show is a bust. One of the influencers has a heart attack, and that kills the buzz. The weather turns heavy and no one goes out. The gallery floods and must be shut down for the plumbers. Reviews are scant. Sales are scanter. The rest of the cold rainy month and half of the next is taken up in futile efforts to force the Hong Kong collector to take his paintings, the gallery's refusal to give him his deposit back, the hiring of lawyers on both sides. The manager's tone in emails to Alex turns frosty.

Alex calls Winter every day until it rings out. Finally, one evening in late August, her friend picks up.

"Are you crying?" Alex asks.

Winter sniffles. "Happy birthday to me."

"I knew that."

"Fuck the fuck off." But she doesn't hang up.

"You're alone?"

"Emma and I are . . . it was off for a while after the miscarriage, but now it's back on. I'm in a motel to give her some space."

Alex is sleeping at her studio pretty much all the time now. She lights up a stale joint found in a drawer and pours vodka into a coffee cup.

"You're giving your partner space on your birthday?"

"Well, the show . . . you know how it is. Nerves and whatnot. Cocaine doesn't help. But everyone does that, right? She goes to this local club to unwind. It's called 'Evo-slash-Lution'. Except the slash is silent of course."

Alex says. "Look, I can be there in a couple of hours. We can sit on the beach and watch the sunrise."

"There's no beach."

139

"A park then."

"Alex. Don't. Please. It won't help. Emma knows I used to have feelings for you."

Used to?

"Plus, I'm pregnant again." And then Winter begins to cry for real.

━╱╲━

Alex feels adrift. She sleeps badly, has dreams of Abby, and wakes ambushed by grief. The rains stop and spring sneaks in. One afternoon in September she is eating a late lunch in the park and finds a review of Emma Ford's work. It describes the emergence of the photographer into the gallery scene as "subverting the artistic tradition of turning the longing gaze against itself".

As Winter would say, *What the absolute fuck?*

A couple strolls into the park and unleashes their kelpie, who streaks past Alex in a russet blur of ribs and teeth. Impossible to capture that on canvas, she thinks, or in any other form—but one day, it'd be fun to try. She can't remember the last time she tried to have fun. Over the years, the need for that, and everything else outside her studio, had become overshadowed by something stronger than need. There seemed to be a wanting in her, a hollow place into which she could crawl, feel its contours settle around her fetal form, take the shape of her own desires, nestle into her hidden places.

The afternoon is getting chilly. The light has turned golden and there is no sign of the kelpie or its owners. She clicks on a new gallery featuring a collection by Emma Ford called 'Tomorrow's Eve'. The subject is Winter, nude or semi-nude and in early pregnancy, her belly swollen and her skin sprinkled with pale freckles luminous as the Milky Way. Alex's heart pounds. Her feet and hands turn to ice. In the background of every photograph is *Homesick #30*—but *not as Alex painted it*. The figure in the attic window of the South Coast cabin is on the move. It is halfway out the window.

But it can't be. Alex zooms in closer. The figure's shoulders jut almost to its ears, and a leg is unmistakably lifted to the sill. There is something wrong with one of the knees.

Alex clicks her phone shut. She looks around the empty park, smells exhaust and hears traffic on the highway. It's rush hour. She

140

doesn't know what to do. Emma must have altered the painting. Some digital process that Alex doesn't know about. But surely Winter will.

She opens the gallery website again. There are a dozen Emma Ford works in that exhibition, all with Winter as the subject, nude or half-dressed in a filmy wedding gown, and all with *Homesick #30* in the background, taking up all the space. Winter is bigger than the painting but uncannily dwarfed by it all the same. Alex slowly zooms in on the image (the gallery has conveniently uploaded them at almost the original resolution) to see that, spilling from one eye of the woman in the beach house, are a blurry stream of corroded crimson ciphers.

Like tears.

From this point everything in her life will separate into a *before* and an *after*, dreaming and waking. At the very moment that she both feels this and moves past the feeling, the phone rings. It's just past 6pm. She's been sitting there for almost two hours, her uneaten sandwich on the bench beside her. It's Winter's phone number, but when she picks it up a stranger's voice says, "Are you Alex Silber?"

It's Emma's neighbor down on the Southern Highlands. Emma is away on location and Winter has gone into early labor.

━╱┃╲━

The freeway snakes southwest towards the Highlands, red taillights swimming. Alex's drives through a tiny shotgun town with a single street of colonial-era buildings and scattered weatherboard cottages. The lights are still on at the pub, but the streets are empty.

The address that the neighbor gave her on the phone is just outside the town. The neighbor greets Alex in the driveway. She wears a terry-cloth bathrobe over gumboots.

"She asked for you," the woman says, as if she can't fathom why. "Ambulance is on its way."

Alex goes into the church. Winter huddles at the foot of a staircase in what was once the foyer to a church. She is deep in the grip of her contractions, her nightgown drawn up over swollen ankles. Alex sinks down and takes her friend into her arms.

The nave has been converted into an open-plan living area, scattered leather furniture and rugs, kitchen and dining to the right. Weak moonlight filters through leadlight windows. But what makes Alex's blood crawl as she strokes Winter's damp head are the black-and-white photographs of *#30* that cover every inch of every wall between the narrow rectangles of glass and the wooden carvings. There must be a hundred. Maybe more. They generate a white heat, like eyes rolled back in their heads.

The neighbor clears her throat. Winter's closed eyelids are webbed in purple veins. Alex brushes the auburn fringe off her forehead, and her hand comes away slick with sweat.

"Burn them, Alex," Winter whispers. "I tried but she stopped me."

"Emma?" Alex says.

A contraction, bad enough to unleash a protracted wail, prevents Winter from answering. The ambulance arrives. She won't let Alex go with her.

"Studio," she rasps. "Tower. Burn it. Burn them all."

The ambulance speeds away. "You art people," says the neighbor, stomping off.

Alex stands alone on the gravel driveway and looks up at the ugly brick converted church Emma inherited from her father. To the rear is a squat bell tower. Beyond the building, the property runs downhill to some woods beyond a small cemetery. Back inside, the room spins around her like a Zoetrope. She feels her eyes bulge painfully. Emma has vandalized the photographs of *Homesick #30* almost to the point of erasure. She's photoshopped obscenities or porn onto some of them, superimposed text and newspaper clippings across the beach house, digitally torn the whole image into shreds and put it back together the wrong way. She's drawn boobs on the figure in the attic window, a moustache in poop, thought bubbles, comic-book *THWACKS!*, cock-and-balls. Some of the photos of the painting are huge, over a meter high; others are small enough to fit into a closed fist. She's used filters—sepia, psychedelic—negative processing, or strange angles—Dutch, longshot, underground, through the ceiling, fish-and birds-eye, under-and overexposed. Out on a ledge and far from home.

It hurts. It hurts a lot.

Winter is right. They must be destroyed. She begins to move toward the wall but freezes at a low gurgle coming from overhead. It rises to a growl, falls to a whisper. The door of the church slams behind her in the wind, surely the wind, although Alex can't shake the feeling of an unwanted presence now in the building with her.

Her heart hammers, and she looks for some escape. The big doors have slammed shut and are too far away for her to get to in time. But to her left, deeply recessed in the wall, is a smaller door, not even as tall as she is. Alex rushes over to it, but it's locked.

No escape from the curse of art.

There is a spiral staircase at the rear near what would have been the altar, which evidently snakes up to the bell tower. This must be the studio. The mutter falls to a single word, whispered again and again.

Alex knows, although she has never heard it spoken before, that it is the fifth word.

Alex claps her hands over her ears. She zigzags across the cowhide rug and bangs her shin against a glass coffee table. She skips the first step of the staircase, hauls herself around two, three steps at a time, leaning on the banister. It's sticky, as if with fresh paint. The air thickens as she winds higher and higher. Darkness gathers and reshapes itself around her like a shroud, and looking down, she can no longer see the floor. The stairs end, or begin, at a rough-hewn rectangular opening. She crawls through using her elbows so as not to touch the sticky edges with her hands. Her knees knife. She smells sulfur. She pushes herself upright. Finally, she emerges in a claustrophobic space converted into a studio.

The muttering has stopped. The silence is heavy, waiting.

The word is

The word is

Pale squares of glass overlook the yard, and above is a skylight webbed by tiny fractures, like something walked across it that shouldn't have. As Alex adjusts to the darkness, she makes out a monitor, laptop, and dormant studio lights. On a worktable is a withered plant, an industrial tape dispenser, and a pile of spent matches. Explaining the smell.

Homesick #30 hangs on the wall above the table. The artist in the window is long gone.

Instead, horribly, something pushes out of the beach house dormer window *in the painting*. Alex goes rigid with fear. It plops gruesomely onto the worktable. Something pushes out after it, and something else after that. Squirming from the actual painting. Worms.

Alex backs up right to the edge of the stairwell through which she crawled. The worms are a brackish red. A bulky shadow at the edge of her eye causes a sudden loosening of her bladder because Alex is certain it sees her back.

The smell of piss is strong.

The shadow jerks forward with the sound of bones splintering and takes on an unmistakable solidity. Another faltering step brings into view a human head atop a shapeless body. Alex sobs, her neck stiff from looking-not-looking. The outlines of the figure sharpen. The broad shoulders kink unevenly. It shifts position with a protracted splintering sound. Over her shoulder, Alex can no longer see no winding staircase, no floor below, just an opening into unrelenting darkness. The figure moves closer, almost upon her. Its arms lift away from the jaunts and angles of its body into the glimmer from the skylight, wanting finally to be seen. Alex makes a strangled, inarticulate cry. The knees are facing the wrong way.

"Aunt Abby?"

At the sound of the name, dead eyes fix on her, round and silver like ball bearings. The hair is long and stringy and seeping.

"N-n-n-ever . . . " begins her aunt, the artist, the witch—in a tongue beyond time.

The woman who is and isn't Abby, Alina, Alona, Ahava, Ariel . . . jerks upright again, knees and back creaking audibly, and suddenly she is on the other side of Alex. Between her and the exit. Alex is trapped—but worse, this creature, this curse, can't be allowed to escape. She promised Winter. She steps backward, her hands fumbling across the worktable and squelching on worms. Her fingers wrap around the tape dispenser. She flings a worm off. It is six inches long and slithers away in a flash of light. She raises the heavy tape dispenser above her head.

" . . . let it go." The words come from the woman in a language that Alex has never heard, and yet she understands it in that part of her that is always dreaming, never fully in the world and never outside it. Suddenly the woman drops on all fours, unleashing a smell like old goat, and scuttles backwards over the edge of the opening, a wet tendril of hair, red as a vein, all that remains. And then it too is gone.

The tape dispenser is still raised above Alex's head. She slowly lowers it; it falls from her fingers onto the floor. Leaning across the seething worktable, she rips the painting off its wire. From the top of the stairwell, she can once again discern the dull spiraling gleam of the railing and the glow of the living area downstairs. Holding the painting under her arm, she half tumbles down the stairs. The small side door that appeared locked earlier was just jammed and she shoulders it open, runs to an open paddock beyond the graveyard. She lights a bonfire and tosses #30 into the flames, hearing the tinkle of exploding glass, smelling solvent. The canvas curls into a ball, the red skin of squirming souls splitting and popping in the flames.

Then she drives back to the hospital and stays with Winter through the C-section. The baby is a blood-and-vernix-smeared bundle of blind need who must go on life support.

At daybreak Alex returns to the property. She takes down every photograph of her painting and burns them all in the bonfire, lest their myopic gaze corrupt in ways her aunt and all the aunts before her knew it would, the curse just waiting for a crack in time to seed its destruction. It takes her until early the next morning, partly because of the dozens of trips she must make back and forth through the low side door, until her knees ache and her throat is raw from the toxic smoke. And partly because of the breaks she takes to cry.

When she returns to the hospital, Emma lies beside Winter on the bed. Emma's hair is the dull steel of a Brillo pad, and tendons bulge on her long neck. Their tiny daughter sleeps in a basinet beside them. Winter sleeps too, but Emma's eyes are open, never letting go.

━╱╻╲━

As soon as Winter is well, there is a combined wedding and Name Day at which Alex is appointed godmother to baby Angelica (*Andzelika* in another time and place). Over the next few weeks, Emma deletes all her files that contain even a fragment of any image of *Homesick #30*—there are thousands of them. It is a bit like those CAPTCHA tests, she quips sadly, not needing Alex to remind her that the dangers of anyone being exposed to any part of *Homesick #30* are unthinkable. That leaves Alex the job of tracking down the buyers of all the Tomorrow Eves. Alex goes through most of her own savings to buy them back, burning each on the pyre in the paddock beneath the wheeling cockatoos. According to Emma's records of sale, there is one remaining painting which Alex is unable to trace. When she asks about the buyer, named Noel Vie, Emma describes him as a flamboyant collector in a greasy suit with dyed hair gelled to stand up on end on his head like little red worms.

"He came in through the Devil's door." Emma points to the small door on the north side of the church, the same door Alex used to ferry her painting to its pyre. Emma explained that it wasn't a real Devil's door—but that's what small doors on the north side of churches are traditionally called. "From the early days of Christianity to let pagan worshippers in, and in Christian rituals like baptisms, to let the Devil out," she says. "He tried to cut a deal."

"The Devil?" Alex asks. "Or the missing buyer?"

"Funny story," Emma says without smiling. "As soon as I saw him, I'm like I literally want to have your baby. He was so perfectly awful that I felt drawn to him immediately. Silly mummy," she clucks at the infant dozing in her arms. "Luckily, the second time he came around he put me off immediately by trying to set the terms." Emma shivers theatrically and Alex can't help but admire the performance, tarnished but with a hammy charm. "*Big* mistake. Art for sperm—come *on!*"

Heat pulses across Alex's chest. "So what did you do?"

"Winter and I agreed to get an anonymous donor—anyone but an artist was okay by her."

"No, I mean with the buyer. Did he come back?"

"Oh yeah. I doubled the price. Said he could keep his seed to himself thanks very much. This was a cash-only deal. So, whatever. He paid it—had to save face—and left the same way he came in."

The Devil's door.

Alex thinks about the one remaining *Tomorrow's Eve* and its owner, and how every time he looks at that painting, he'll be reminded of the one who got away and how after all, that might not be such a bad thing.

She lets it go.

━╱╿╲━

The morning sky is still pink, overhung with slate blue clouds reflected in the tide. Alex stands at the dormer window in the attic she has converted into a studio. The stairs are a killer on her knees, but the light-filled space is worth it. Necessary you might say. It's Saturday, the day that Angelica arrives from Sydney by train to spend the weekend with her aunt. Angel, as she likes to be known, is thirteen, and Alex's days with the girl are numbered. It isn't just that Emma is protective over the child, who isn't strong. Nor is it that Winter, who has reluctantly agreed to part with her daughter each week for Alex's sake, is beginning to think of excuses to keep her away—there are better things for a teenage girl to be doing than hanging with her antisocial Godmother. Soon it will be once a month, and then only over the summer, and then it will be nothing until the child decides to come back of her own accord, as Alex hopes, and fears, that she must.

Alex has seen a shadow over the girl's shadow.

Winter has not been to the beach house for some months, and Alex is glad that her old friend can't see her like this, can't see that however much she reassures Winter, this—what is happening to her body and her mind—is the curse, the price that all the aunts going back to that village in Poland agreed to pay in return for a chance to right wrongs. To balance the darkness with light. To balance fear with love.

Was there ever a true artist not cursed with both?

Angel waves up at her godmother in the window, and Alex waves back against the pain in her joints, against the crookedness of her arms, against how her legs sometimes feel, as they do today, like they're screwed on backwards. A scream pulls her lips back in a rictus of a smile. Her eyes bulge and fill with blood. On days like this she is gripped, as Abby must have been, and Alina and Alona, Aviva and Alaya and Ariel too, and Ahava Zilberman and the very first aunt, whoever she was, with an impulse to warn love away, to open the window and call, "Turn back, child. Back! Your mothers are right, as mothers often but not always are. Art wants what it wants and the cost is more than you can pay!"

And as Angel gets closer, she falters, as if she's heard the unspoken warning in a hidden part of herself. Beneath her raven fringe, her brow creases and her smile quivers. But she is almost at the threshold now, that place of surrender. So Alex swallows the cry and calls to the child to let herself in. Sweat cools on her skin and the swelling in her joints begins to subside as soon as she reaches her easel. Art is the power and the letting go of power. It is the beginning and the end of all hope. She pours lemon cordial into two tall glasses, adds ice, and in hers, sloshes some 666 Pure, a high-end Tasmanian vodka gifted from an appreciative collector. Two of her paintings have just been bought by the National Gallery for its permanent collection—she has put the money away for Angel's education—art school, maybe? She takes up a fine brush and dips it in silver, cadmium red at the ready. The work is her latest in a new series called 'Lovesick'. It is of the bay at sunrise, and the paint on the waves is still sticky to the touch.

SEASICK

Angel crossed the Strip at twilight. Billboards glowed and neon popped as if surprised at its own existence. She passed by the dollar store and the tattoo parlor. Hiro wasn't working today, so there was no point in going in, and she was late for her real job—real because it covered regular hours and included insurance. She slowed past Barley Café where people were typing on their Great American whatevers, energized by jackfruit tacos and single-origin lattés. She picked up her pace and ducked into the bookstore just on the dot of five. Her boss, Marcus was behind the counter looking particularly grumpy, so she edged between the Moleskine stand and the Staff Picks shelf and headed to the café.

An hour into her shift and a video text came through from Stevie showing little Eva and Joey dancing, running in circles and flapping their arms up and down to Radiohead's *Karma Police*.

Angel texted back, *There's a good nursery rhymes playlist on my iPad. Just saying.*

But it was hard to tell Stevie how to do anything. Angel supposed that a trip down her friend's musical memory lane couldn't hurt the twins too much. Let it go. Like her therapist said, *Neither sought nor feared, pain can transform us when it has a purpose.*

Tonight's reading was almost over and the sparse crowd of locals, family, roommates and even one or two actual book buyers would be hitting the bar any moment. Angel untied her apron and said she had to go to the bathroom. She ducked her head out the back door to see how the reading was going. The small audience sat beneath string lights looped back and forth across the courtyard. The author, Josh Leary, stood with his back to a large mural—a multi-armed dreaming demon that looked, in the rippling light, as if it floated in space. The reading was over; question time had begun. Leary lived locally. He was crying-laughing, and his people in the audience—all six of them—were crying-laughing too.

Stevie had an MFA, and had told Angel how her professor had said that every sentence should be as clear as a grizzly bear in a brightly lit kitchen. Something caught Angel's eye; a dark shape that didn't belong. The shape was human male-ish, lean and bear-high, right by the exit to the parking lot, and just beyond the glow of the lights. Keeping the bear shape at the side of her eye, she watched the red bead of his cigarette float up and down, and she was gripped by the shakes.

"Someone step on your grave?" grumbled Marcus behind her.

Before she could think of a suitably jaunty reply, Marcus had stepped outside and was piling up Josh's unsold books. Australians were casual and goofy with each other, but Marcus, like so many Angelinos she'd met, was opaque. She needed this job. And Angel sucked at jaunty. So instead, she just asked about the unknown guest, but by the time Marcus looked to where Angel was pointing, the bear-shaped man was gone.

➤ ⁄ ❭ ◀

Angel was a little out of breath from hurrying home after her shift, about a fifteen-minute walk up Laveta Terrace. She raced in to check on the twins before saying hello to Stevie. They were fast asleep, the nightlight sending ghostly shoals of fish, octopi, and baby whales, across the walls.

"How was the reading?" Stevie was tapping at her laptop, her wig askew.

Angel still felt unable to shake the unease that had niggled at her since seeing the stranger smoking against the wall, but why worry Stevie? "Cute," Angel said. "You writing up the review?"

Stevie worked at the LA Review of Books. But she shook her head. "Opus," she said. "So close to the end, and yet so far."

Stevie had been working on her Great American screenplay ever since they'd known each other—since before the twins were born.

"What was cute about it?" Stevie asked.

"Just the usual. Everyone cried."

"Tears don't pay the rent," Stevie said, meaning she'd be giving Josh the full five stars.

Angel was glad she spent pretty much all of Aunt Alex's "education" fund moving to LA, then getting a good OB-GYN for the twins and paying for Stevie's surgery and treatment in return for babysitting, but mainly in return for the friendship. She missed her mums, and knew she was probably a disappointment to them, even though Emma especially had encouraged her to get out of Sydney for a while. "There's a real world out there," she'd said. "Go and figure out what it wants from you."

Mama Emma's posture was still dancer-perfect in middle age, her neck impossibly long, white hair pulled up in a bun. She once had some kind of creative destiny mapped out for Angel, but her mum, Winter, said she couldn't care less if her daughter didn't have a creative bone in her body.

"Life's easier that way," Winter had said. "Creatives drink too much."

"They do everything too much." Emma planted a kiss on Winter's forehead. It had been nice to see her mums happy again after everything they'd gone through.

"Promise that you'll leave enough of Aunt Alex's money for plane fare home. Just in case," Winter said, and Angel promised.

Winter had a thing about drinking because of Aunt Alex's dissipation. She'd always smell Angel's breath after one of her regular painting weekends down south with her aunt, who was really her godmother.

But after the kidnapping, the visits stopped.

The first time she talked about it was to Stevie. And the second was in therapy, to get well for her unborn children.

I was kidnapped at fourteen.

She'd been holding those five words in so long it didn't even sound like her voice.

Stay with that feeling. That fear, the therapist said. But that was asking too much.

➤➤➤

"I heard that Aimee Bender is launching her new book here next week," yawned Stevie, packing up her things. "Maybe we can all go."

Angel slept with the twins that night. When the dreams finally took her, she was back at the beach house with Aunt Alex, who was leaning tipsily into her easel, the better to conceal some silver curse in the wicked curls of the incoming tide.

➤/ \ ◄

The next morning, Angel and the twins popped into El Classico Tattoos because Hiro was on, and there were no customers yet. It was still early, the mist not yet dissipated. Angel was headed to the Farmer's Market.

"They got me on the dud shift as usual," Hiro said, kneeling down in front of the double stroller and passing them his hat to play with. Hiro's tousled hair was flecked with silver, sexy as fuck. Angel didn't know who or what Hiro was into that way. And anyway, after six years in LA, she was just looking for a friend. Hiro wasn't family like Stevie had become, but he was exhausted and adrift like Angel, and far from home. Plus, the owner hated him, and instead of giving him the busy shifts on a Friday or Saturday night, put him on Sunday morning. Angel just worked there two evenings a week, but that was enough for her to see that the reason the owner hated him was because Hiro was a true artist and the owner wasn't. Hiro's art was wild, especially when it came to color. Sick yellows and lavenders and a red so raw, so pure it hurt. Last count, Angel had eleven tattoos, six of which were Hiro's—on her back, the spreading oak tree overhung with moss that Eva loved, a swan and a goat on her thigh, a weird Japanese Little Red Riding hood heading into the forest that was Joey's favorite, random butterflies on her belly, and on her shoulder—her mums' names in a heart; and Eva and Joey's too—in cursive on the outside of her right forearm between the point and the nock of a delicate arrow. She'd never been able to bring herself to get anything that reminded her of Aunt Alex, or the house by the beach that Angel once loved, once thought of as safe.

But getting kidnapped changed all that. It changed everything.

The doorbell tinkled and a customer walked in, still drunk from the night before. A New Zealand tourist in a Quicksilver T-shirt. He chose a double-rose and skull design and asked for a private room.

—⟋⟍—

The launch the following Saturday night, was standing room only. The buzz and the sales were too good to let even the cost of extra catering staff put Marcus in a bad mood. Angel bought the new book and was waiting for an opportunity to get it signed as a gift for Emma, who was a huge Aimiee Bender fan. Marcus set up a bar in the courtyard, and Angel was pouring her hundredth malbec, her eyes no longer focusing on faces, just hands open to wrap themselves around cups and stuff bills in the tip jar.

"I'd kill for a bourbon, girl," a deep, melodic voice said in her ear. "When do you finish?"

It was Stevie, wearing a Zadie Smith head-wrap. "Not forever," Angel said. "Did you get some good shots for the feature?"

Because Stevie was doing a big feature on the launch, Angel had had to get a regular sitter—an oncology nurse who Stevie knew, but Angel had only met once.

"Chill," Stevie said. "They'll be fine."

But then Hiro came up to the table, and Josh and some other locals. Josh opened his jacket to reveal a fifth of honey bourbon, and Angel gave them a stack of paper cups and then checked her phone again to see if the sitter had answered her text. She was just about to call, when Marcus came up to the table to clear away cups.

"No phones," he said. "You want a break, take one."

Angel gave him a bold but grateful grin which he didn't return. Feeling idiotic but with a knot of panic in her gut that she couldn't ignore, she went out to the parking lot to make the call. It rang out and she was about to try Messenger when a shadow fell over her shaking hands, and the glow of the screen faded to black. Angel smelled smoke. She looked up at the unforgettable silhouette, and this time when unconsciousness took her, she was back in an airless attic waiting to die.

—⟋⟍—

He hadn't touched her, not after he'd lured her to his car with a hurt dog and stuffed her in the trunk. She woke up in that attic— only knowing it was an attic because of the steps she heard him climb to bring her food and change the chemical toilet. It was a lightless space, crammed with junk and shadows she could barely make out—dust covered storage boxes and what looked like an animal crate, and books. He'd crammed a camp bed sideways in front of a brick chimney that heated up the whole space, made her lethargic and lightheaded.

Hanging from a nail on the chimney was a framed photograph. The photography was Emma's style, all silvery and stark, but Angel had never seen it before. The subject was her mum, Winter, pregnant with Angel, and in the background was a large painting of a house, that looked like something weird and dark that Aunt Alex would do. Angel had the impression that Emma had done something to the photograph that magnified the painting somehow, making it look bigger than it was. Either way it was in focus, while her mother, Winter, was a little blurred in the foreground. The painting was of a beach house with a smashed roof open to the soot-black sky.

Angel backed away from it as from a snake. But he made her look. When she refused, he made her. She didn't know how—he would stand in the shadows taking up too much space and not enough. She didn't always hear him come up, or know he was there. He didn't open his mouth, not once, but just sent thoughts into her head. Terrible thoughts. And the thoughts made her look at the painting, and every time she looked, it changed.

And so, over time, did she.

"It's your mother's work," her kidnapper said without moving his mouth, the words worming into her head. "Powerful, isn't it? You think it can't see you back. But you're dead wrong. It sees you, Angel. It wants you. And you want it back."

She had tried to block out his words by looking for his reflection in the framed photograph. Once or twice she glimpsed the looming shadow he made on the walls—Stevie-Rotten spiked hair and skinny as hell.

"Most kidnappings are done by a friend or relative of the victim," she'd read once. What part of their lives—Emma's and Winter's and Alex's—had she gotten tangled up in? Whose friend was her kidnapper? Whose enemy? In the end she didn't care. She made a promise to herself. That if she ever got out of this attic alive, she'd get as far the fuck away as she could, from all of them.

Sunday after the book launch. Angel made pancakes for the kids. Stevie came over before taking her cancer medication, while she could still eat.

"You okay?" she asked Angel, because she hated anyone making a fuss about the chemo. It was like giving it a name made it real.

"Do you think I still have a job?" Angel said.

Stevie said with a mouth full of maple syrup, "Marcus was cool. We took care of it."

And by "we" Angel knows it was Stevie. Stevie, who hadn't let Angel out of her sight, not even with a big launch to cover. Stevie who'd come out to check on her when she hadn't returned to the table. And Stevie who found her where she fell.

"What happened, Angel? Who did you see?"

Stay in that place of fear, the therapist said. *Stay with the feeling.*

"I think it was the guy who kidnapped me when I was a kid. I think he was there."

"What, wait? Didn't you say you—he died, right?"

Angel nodded, put down her fork. "The authorities found the body, but there was some confusion."

"You told me you IDed him?"

"I said it was him."

"Seriously? You weren't sure?"

Lying in wait behind the attic door, she'd made a run for it, and he'd caught her at the top of the landing. His arms coiled around her like electrical wire sizzling with heat. Her flesh blistered at his touch. She screamed, fought him with every instinct she possessed and a strength she didn't know she had. But he held on, the reek of burning meat. Her legs kicked in the air; she slapped at his balaclava-ed face and beat against his scarecrow chest. In the struggle they got turned around, Do-si-do and away we go. They staggered like dancers, like lovers, the balaclava pulling up to expose his chin, flesh the color and texture of gesso. The staircase was now at his back. Angel gripped the banister, managed to get a knee to his groin. His junk felt as hollow as the rest of him. He'd let go then, collapsed in on himself and fell backward, heels-over-head, all the way down.

Even then, with him lying crumpled at a weird angle at the foot of the stairs, Angel had been careful not to look at where the balaclava had slipped from his face. Careful—as she crept down the stairs and stepped over him—not to remember anything about the house he'd taken her to. Careful to keep her eyes on the door, on the beginning of escape.

"He was a goner. I killed him. I've had years of therapy trying to deal with it."

She got up and wiped the twin's faces. Set them in front of cartoons, a Sunday treat.

"You mean trying to deal with the possibility that the guy you *thought* was dead, maybe wasn't?" Stevie said, pouring another coffee. "Maybe he just got up after you escape, took a stiff from his serial-killer's collection, or picked some loser off the street and broke his neck, and did the old switcheroo. How would the cops know any different? How would *you*, if you hadn't seen his face for real?"

"Oh God. Shut up. Stevie. The kids."

Stevie leaned forward and rasped in a stage-whisper, "Based on you not being crazy *and* convinced enough that the guy at the bookstore was him, all I'm saying is that the body the cops later found might not have been the same one that fell down the stairs."

"That I pushed, you mean."

"Or sometime later at the morgue or whatever it got up and—"

"What the absolute fuck, Stevie?"

When Angel had first confided in Stevie, she'd been grateful that her friend believed her, had agreed that there were things about what happened that couldn't be explained. Like the burn scars around her arms that she had to tattoo over. But hearing her deepest fears thrown back at her like this, that there was something about who took her, and what, that she might never, in this world, escape—that was too much.

"Mommy?" Joey stood up on the couch, facing her. "I'm hungry."

Angel stood up. "Park o'clock!" She clapped like a teacher. No one moved.

"Sit down," Stevie said. "Didn't your aunt, the batshit crazy artist, have a thing about a family curse?"

"My mums never let me visit her alone again. They didn't forgive her for not watching me, not being able to protect me," Angel slumped back down in her chair. "But it was my fault. I ran off. I ran away from her."

Stevie took a deep, impatient breath. "Hold up. Wasn't she into curses and sorcery and such?"

Angel had once asked Alex if she'd trade it all in—the fame, the genius, the rush of art, for a chance to go back in time and stop that long-ago uncle who got this whole ball of suck rolling. *May as well ask how long is a piece of string*, was Alex's only answer which was no answer at all. Angel closed her eyes. She didn't like to think about it, had tried to forget the words Aunt Alex had tried to teach her, the red and silver symbols that made her feel like throwing up, like hurting herself or someone else. "She was just sick, living in some fantasy world. I should have called, even if they wouldn't let me visit. She gave me all this money for school. I took it and got the hell out."

"Let it go."

Eva was standing on the couch now. "Mommy?"

Joey sunk back down and started sucking his thumb.

"All I'm saying," Stevie lowered her voice, "is maybe call her. It's never too late."

"Isn't it?"

Since the kidnapping, the photograph in the attic had appeared in her dreams, and sometimes when she wasn't dreaming, making her feel like she was. Making her feel bad things. Twisting her perception, so she sometimes thought about hurting people. But more often herself. She began to feel pressed up against a fragile membrane beyond which she could just make out a yearning space so dark and vast that not even the tattoos or cutting her bangs or cutting herself, gave her relief from the want. For what, she didn't know, or couldn't name. Except that it was terrible. And also beautiful. And then, one night at Burning Man (or was it Vegas) she made the twins.

After that the dreams stopped.

"Call Not-Aunt Alex," Stevie said. "It's time."

⚊⟋⟨⟋⚊

Which is how Angel ended up Skyping with her Godmother that night after putting the twins to bed. Alex asking her if she remembered the five words of the curse-slash-blessing.

How could Angel not?

"And remember—the first four in silver, and the fifth in red?" Alex said.

156

"So, you think it's him then, the guy I saw at the bookstore?" Angel asked. "That he was never . . . "

"Dead?"

"And that he's found me again?" Angel's whisper was more like a hiss. "Is that what you think?"

Alex was still a presence, even on screen. Her coarse black hair framed a narrow face with large eyes that glimmered with held-back tears. "I think it was a mistake not to go after that final buyer of your mother's photographs—the one who came in through the Devil's door. He found you in the end. Which wasn't the end."

Which was pretty much how Aunt Alex always talked.

"When?" Angel pleaded, regretting the call, knowing it was too late for regret. "When will it end?"

Alex lifted a glass of vodka and her face froze in a software glitch, her mouth in a grimace, one eye bulging, the other smeared across the screen. Her hair aureoled by coastal light washing in through the attic window.

"Not when," Angel said. "But who. It must end with you. It was always going to be you . . . "

"Why me?"

" . . . and not on a canvas, but on your flesh."

"Wait, what?"

"You refused art. You resisted its pull. You were the first. At the time I was relieved. Hopeful even, that you'd been spared. But I was wrong. What kind of curse would it be if it answered my prayers? I imagine that short time in the attic exposed to the painting was enough to infect you with the disease. But not the same as the rest of us, for some reason, and so maybe there's hope."

Alex's words were coming through loud and clear, but her image had gone grainy, as if behind a window in the rain.

"Hope?" Was there ever an artist without it? "How?"

"Maybe because instead of becoming an artist," Alex said, "you became a work of art."

The ink crawled beneath Angel's flesh: the tattoos wriggling and squirming and slithering.

"Why?" she pleaded. "Why me?"

"No escape," Alex shrugged. "Except through change. If the curse can't be undone, maybe it can be transformed, again. And who knows into what this time. But I think, Angel, that it's time to try."

The morning before the kidnapping, Alex had told Angel that this must be her last visit, that she had a bad feeling, had seen a shadow over Angel's shadow. Angel had cried, hurt, thought it was because she wasn't a true artist and was a disappointment to her adored Godmother. She'd run out of the house, and down the beach. Alex had called after her to come back, that it was raining, but Angel kept going. She ran as far as the surf club and into the arms of her kidnapper. He was standing by his car in the parking lot, and wore a hoody. Medicine-red hair poking under the fold.

"Can you wait a second while I check on the kids?" Angel asked. It wasn't that she really needed to, but more just to gather her thoughts. She stood at the threshold of their bedroom, the nightlight washing stars across their little clenched fists. She stopped in the kitchen on the way back and poured herself a drink.

"What should I do, Alex?" she asked sitting back down in front of the screen.

"Your flesh is your canvas, Angel. Find an artist, a good one, who will tattoo the first four words in silver, and then quickly, the fifth in red. Somewhere on your body hidden in plain sight. Conceal the words in a larger design. And Angel? Make it your last."

It sounded crazy; it was crazy.

"What if it doesn't work?" Angel asked.

Alex didn't say anything for a while. Angel sipped her vodka, listened to the restless city wail and heave outside her window, the ticking of a clock from the kitchen.

"I've got kids, Aunt Alex. You need to be clear on the risks here."

"You know the risks."

And because Alex spoke the last bit very softly, almost a mumble, Angel's chest felt caught in a vice.

"Eva and Joey saved my life, Aunt Alex."

"I won't let anything happen to them."

Is that what she told Winter and Emma? Is that what this is about, maybe. Even just a little bit? Redemption, a last bid for the artist's soul? Tears glistened on Alex's cheek. She knuckled one off the tip of her nose.

Angel breathed in and out as slowly as she could, taking the air in through her nose and holding it a moment before letting it escape from her mouth, like the therapist said. The last time she felt this kind of panic was in her kidnapper's attic. Is that what the curse does, hold their souls to ransom, hers and Alex's, and all the aunts and nieces before that, going back two centuries to some old hag in the woods who started it all? The first not-aunt.

Which makes her the final niece, maybe. Better be, Angel thought, because that's a title too shitty even for Netflix.

"My Aunt Abby believed in the possibility that the blessing would weaken the curse over time." Alex spun the glass in her paint-stained fingers. A cat jumped up on her lap, a fat green-eyed tabby. It settled just off-camera, its tail twitching at the bottom of the screen. "I've come to realize that weak is not enough. Some things take power in their weakness. But what if the blessing were written on human flesh? It would take on the strength of that humanity, maybe enough to consume the curse in light. And in love."

"Unless it consumes me in septicemia first."

"Find an artist who can work quickly, child. Someone you trust."

Angel felt violently spent, the weekend's stress catching up to her. She downed the vodka, at the precise moment that Alex did the same, twelve thousand kilometers away.

"The fifth word, Aunt Alex, the red one? I always meant to ask what it meant."

"You already know, Angel. You always have."

━╱╿╲━

When Angel explained the process to Hiro, he said no. Tattoo the five words first, he said, and *then* conceal them in the design.

"The design first," she shook her head. "Has to be that way. And just before the design is finished, before the shading, *then* the words, first four in silver and the fifth in red."

How it's always been done. Inscribe the words into a still wet canvas, that they may be concealed just before the point of erasure.

"There's no silver ink, Angel. You know that."

"Grey then. With highlights. Dark grey or black—anything just to create the illusion of it being metallic. And Hiro? Timing is everything."

Of course, she didn't explain why to Hiro. With any luck, she wouldn't need to.

159

"What do the words mean?" he asked, frowning at where she'd scrawled them on a scrap of paper.

"Made up mumbo-jumbo for all I know. This one's for my aunt, Hiro. Please?"

Before she left the apartment, Angel had asked Stevie to take the kids should anything happen. She'd hugged them, the sweaty, squirming bodies pushing into hers. Eva's fingers were like butterfly wings on her neck, Joey's violet eyes searching her face.

"Just don't tell anyone that it's one of mine," he said. "Because it's going to look like freeze-dried roadkill."

His fearlessness gave her heart. Hiro blocked out the position of the five words on her left inner forearm, as small a space as possible, Angel reminded him, the better to conceal them in the wave.

"Hurry," she said, anxious to tear the scrap of paper into shreds.

When he was done, he showed her the catalogue, disappearing into a back room while she leafed through it. She heard music come on.

It took Angel no time at all to decide.

This one, she said when he came back out, pointing to a large tattoo of an ocean swell cresting in a single wave in indigos and blues with a touch of sea-green fading out at either end. She told him to do it on her inner left forearm.

"The last wave," Hiro said, looking at his watch. "That'll take four hours. You won't be able to go the distance in one night."

"Try me. Whatever it costs."

"No way," he said.

"Name your price, Hiro. I mean it. You're about due for trip home, aren't you?"

The lights on the strip were popping, washing Hiro's hat brim in rainbows.

"It'll hurt like hell over the fold, Angel." He traced a finger from the inside of her elbow to just shy of her wrist, his caress more arousing than it should have been.

Neither sought nor feared, pain can transform us when it has a purpose.

Hiro stenciled the wave on her inner arm and he made them both tea while it dried. He applied the A&D and then took a liner to the swell, using a blue-black, beginning with the first faint shape of the big wave as it built from the fold of her arm. Angel's many tattoos hadn't prepared her for the pain—like someone raking a fork under her flesh. He continued with the outline, floating the needle over her skin from which the ghost wave began to emerge. Altering the voltage, he changed to a shader for the greys and blues, some sea greens, the color fading out near her wrist. The free-written words were still just visible under the rise and fall of the swell, part stencil, part shading.

He pushed his hat off his forehead, sat back on the stool.

And there it was. The last wave. Ghosting out from under her skin where it had been waiting all her life.

She shoved the scrap of paper under his nose. "I've memorized them," he said, and tore it up.

Then he flicked on a ring light and began on the first four words, using a single needle to ink them in Titanium Silver. It was really just grey-tinted white, but it was the closest thing to silver, and it would darken when finished. The needle bit like a bitch. At the fourth group of symbols, the final word in the curse, Hiro had to stop to puke in the sink. The room grew dark.

"It's magic, isn't it?" he asked, wiping his mouth. "You could have told me."

"I'm sorry," she said, but then her other tattoos began to sting, a bone-deep burn that swelled to an unbearable seething beneath her skin. A squirming—the ink alive and rippling. Her whole body convulsed. A row of bottles exploded on a shelf, colors running down the wall. She made Hiro strap her arm to the chair so he could hold her skin taut between his own trembling fingers. Sweat stood out in trembling buds of moisture on his forehead. The roar of the traffic outside had become beastly.

Shadows on the wall juddered. They were pointed like thorns. The thorns grew into worms and the worms reached for her.

Angel screamed.

"I can't do this," Hiro said in a voice coming from far away.

She cursed him, took it back, pleading.

"The fifth word," she said. "Now!"

The tattoo was red and raw around the edges. The artery that ran from her elbow to her wrist throbbed, and slowly opened into a terrible smile that cannibalized itself the wider it grinned. Hiro's machine snickered and flew from his fingers.

Joey, Eva, Joa, Evey, Yeeva, Ejay, . . . the names of the twins running into each other, unspeakable, and yet spoken in a voice that growled and moaned from the shadows.

"Never in your mouth!" she screamed at the thorned shadow. "The names of my children never on your tongue."

Hiro tore off his hat and threw it against the wall, bellowed something at the ceiling in Japanese. And then he wiped drool off his mouth and took up another machine. A light blew out. He turned on his phone torch and fastened it around his head with duct tape. Then he took up that raw vermillion, like blood, like love. And he started on the fifth word.

The ciphers morphing before her eyes, beneath Hiro's machine, into four sigils, the ones that Alex showed her long ago. But now she could see them for what they were, and the fifth word, the blessing, for what it was.

l-o-v-e.

And then slowly the roar subsided, and sullenly, the shadows receded. And the wound at her wrist quivered closed.

They were both crying.

Hiro began work on the blending. He changed back to a round shader and extended the first silver word into a charcoal indigo shadow of the wave where it grew out of the ocean on the inside of her elbow. Angel sobbed uncontrollably on a sea of pain. The second word was just off the fold and that hurt less; he turned it into a shadow lurking under the breaker. Each of the four clumps of ciphers, he concealed in the chiaroscuro of the wave, dark and light, moving the needle in tight circles and then wiping, stretching her skin so tight she thought it was going to split. Finally he took up his signature saffron yellow (*temple yellow,* she thought), pepper-shading it around the fifth word, the one she'd always known. And together the vermillion and the yellow blended into something new, a color Angel had never seen before.

"Tequila sunset," Hiro whispered. "Kind of."

Once the first layer of concealment was done, he filled in the wave with dove greys and greens, a lavender like Winter's eyes, deep indigos and blacks, gently swiping at Angel's arm with a moist cloth, dipping the needle in the colors, a far-off radio playing. He finished with highlights, white like Emma's hair, where the wave frothed and broke. Because he had to go back to a liner needle for that, the white light hurt most of all.

And then it was done. It had taken six hours.

"It doesn't look like roadkill to me," she said. The invocation all but concealed in the crashing foaming roll of the wave, unless you knew what you were looking for.

Hiro bent down to pick up his hat. "Not drowning, waving," he said with a shaky laugh.

Angel transferred the money into his account, leaving just enough in her trust fund for emergencies and for the plane fares back to Sydney. Hiro came out of the backroom with a bottle of the boss's whisky and two glasses. She apologized again for not telling him about the curse, and when he said he would have done the same with that kind of magic, she believed him. They promised to visit each other in Tokyo and in Sydney.

When she emerged onto the street, there was a blush on the horizon and the smell of moisture in the air. A delivery truck was already parked outside Barley Café, unloading sacks of hemp flour and coconuts. The driver looked up from his trolley and nodded at her, the streetlamp making a deuce of his shadow. At the traffic lights, she brought a finger to the wave beneath the cling wrap on her arm. She didn't quite touch it—she told herself it was still too sore. It was beautiful, though, a word that had always meant something to Angel. And always would.

Then the lights changed, and she moved on.

DARK
TIDE

Subscribe to Crystal Lake Publishing's
Dark Tide series for updates, specials,
behind-the-scenes content, and a
special selection of bonus stories
- http://eepurl.com/hKVGkr

THE END?

Not if you want to dive into more of the Dark Tide series.

Check out our amazing website and online store
or download our latest catalog here.
https://geni.us/CLPCatalog

Looking for award-winning Dark Fiction?

Download our latest catalog.

Includes our anthologies, novels, novellas, collections,
poetry, non-fiction, and specialty projects.

TALES FROM THE DARKEST DEPTHS

We always have great new projects and content on the website to dive into, as well as a newsletter, behind the scenes options, social media platforms, our own dark fiction shared-world series and our very own webstore. Our webstore even has categories specifically for KU books, non-fiction, anthologies, and of course more novels and novellas.

Our Dark Tide series of novella anthologies

ABOUT THE AUTHORS

Shirley Jackson award-winner **Kaaron Warren** published her first short story in 1993 and has had fiction in print every year since. She was recently given the Peter McNamara Lifetime Achievement Award and was Guest of Honour at World Fantasy 2018, Stokercon 2019 and Geysercon 2019. She has also been Guest of Honour at Conflux in Canberra and Genrecon in Brisbane.

She has published five multi-award winning novels (*Slights, Walking the Tree, Mistification, The Grief Hole* and *Tide of Stone*) and seven short story collections, including *The Gate Theory*. Her most recent novella, Into Bones Like Oil was shortlisted for a Shirley Jackson Award and the Bram Stoker Award, winning the Aurealis Award. Her stories have appeared in both Ellen Datlow's and Paula Guran's *Year's Best* anthologies.

Kaaron was a Fellow at the Museum for Australian Democracy, where she researched prime ministers, artists and serial killers. In 2018 she was Established Artist in Residence at Katharine Susannah Prichard House in Western Australia. She is one part of the popular podcast Let The Cat In and her most recent book is the award-winning writing chapbook, Capturing Ghosts.

Author, artist, and filmmaker, **Aaron Dries** was born and raised in New South Wales, Australia. His novels include the award-winning *House of Sighs, The Fallen Boys, A Place For Sinners, Where The Dead Go To Die* (with Mark Allan Gunnells), and the Shirley Jackson award-nominated novella, *Dirty Heads*. His critically-lauded collection, *Cut To Care*, was described by author Paul Tremblay as "heartbreaking, frightening, and all too real". Dries is one host of the popular podcast, Let The Cat In, and also co-founded Elsewhere Here Productions. His fiction, art, and films have been celebrated both domestically and abroad, and he is currently at work on a new novel. Contact Aaron Dries on TikTok @aarondries_writer or Twitter @AaronDries.

J.S. Breukelaar is an Australian-American author living in Sydney. She is the author of three novels, most recently *The Bridge, Aletheia*, and the Shirley Jackson nominated and Aurealis Award winning, *Collision: Stories*, in addition to essays, poems and fiction appearing in The Dark, Black Static, Lightspeed, Fantasy Mag, and numerous others including several Years Bests. Her work has won or been a finalist for multiple national and international awards, including the Shirley Jackson, Aurealis and Ditmar Awards. She teaches at the University of Western Sydney, LitReactor.com and elsewhere you can also find her at www.thelivingsuitcase.com and on media at @jsbbreukelaar.

Readers . . .

Thank you for reading *Vandal* We hope you enjoyed this 6th book in our Dark Tide series.

If you have a moment, please review *Vandal* at the store where you bought it.

Help other readers by telling them why you enjoyed this book. No need to write an in-depth discussion. Even a single sentence will be greatly appreciated. Reviews go a long way to helping a book sell, and is great for an author's career. It'll also help us to continue publishing quality books. You can also share a photo of yourself holding this book with the hashtag #IGotMyCLPBook!

Thank you again for taking the time to journey with Crystal Lake Publishing.

Visit our Linktree page for a list of our social media platforms. https://linktr.ee/CrystalLakePublishing

Our Mission Statement:

Since its founding in August 2012, Crystal Lake Publishing has quickly become one of the world's leading publishers of Dark Fiction and Horror books in print, eBook, and audio formats.

While we strive to present only the highest quality fiction and entertainment, we also endeavour to support authors along their writing journey. We offer our time and experience in non-fiction projects, as well as author mentoring and services, at competitive prices.

With several Bram Stoker Award wins and many other wins and nominations (including the HWA's Specialty Press Award), Crystal Lake Publishing puts integrity, honor, and respect at the forefront of our publishing operations.

We strive for each book and outreach program we spearhead to not only entertain and touch or comment on issues that affect our readers, but also to strengthen and support the Dark Fiction field and its authors.

Not only do we find and publish authors we believe are destined for greatness, but we strive to work with men and woman who endeavour to be decent human beings who care more for others than themselves, while still being hard working, driven, and passionate artists and storytellers.

Crystal Lake Publishing is and will always be a beacon of what passion and dedication, combined with overwhelming teamwork and respect, can accomplish. We endeavour to know each and every one of our readers, while building personal relationships with our authors, reviewers, bloggers, podcasters, bookstores, and libraries.

We will be as trustworthy, forthright, and transparent as any business can be, while also keeping most of the headaches away from our authors, since it's our job to solve the problems so they can stay in a creative mind. Which of course also means paying our authors.

We do not just publish books, we present to you worlds within your world, doors within your mind, from talented authors who sacrifice so much for a moment of your time.

There are some amazing small presses out there, and through collaboration and open forums we will continue to support other presses in the goal of helping authors and showing the world what quality small presses are capable of accomplishing. No one wins when a small press goes down, so we will always be there to support hardworking, legitimate presses and their authors. We don't see Crystal Lake as the best press out there, but we will always strive to be the best, strive to be the most interactive and grateful, and even blessed press around. No matter what happens over time, we will also take our mission very seriously while appreciating where we are and enjoying the journey.

What do we offer our authors that they can't do for themselves through self-publishing?

We are big supporters of self-publishing (especially hybrid publishing), if done with care, patience, and planning. However, not every author has the time or inclination to do market research, advertise, and set up book launch strategies. Although a lot of authors are successful in doing it all, strong small presses will always be there for the authors who just want to do what they do best: write.

What we offer is experience, industry knowledge, contacts and trust built up over years. And due to our strong brand and trusting fanbase, every Crystal Lake Publishing book comes with weight of respect. In time our fans begin to trust our judgment and will try a new author purely based on our support of said author.

With each launch we strive to fine-tune our approach, learn from our mistakes, and increase our reach. We continue to assure our authors that we're here for them and that we'll carry the weight of the launch and dealing with third parties while they focus on their strengths—be it writing, interviews, blogs, signings, etc.

We also offer several mentoring packages to authors that include knowledge and skills they can use in both traditional and self-publishing endeavours.

We look forward to launching many new careers.

This is what we believe in. What we stand for. This will be our legacy.

Welcome to Crystal Lake Publishing— Tales from the Darkest Depths.

Manufactured by Amazon.com.au
Sydney, New South Wales, Australia